TOBY WHEELER

Eighth-Grade Benchwarmer

TOBY WHEELER

Eighth-Grade Benchwarmer

THATCHER HELDRING

DELACORTE PRESS

Published by Delacorte Press
an imprint of Random House Children's Books
a division of Random House, Inc.
New York

Delacorte Press and colophon are registered trademarks
of Random House, Inc.

www.randomhouse.com/kids
Educators and librarians, for a variety of teaching tools,
visit us at www.randomhouse.com/teachers

Library of Congress Cataloging-in-Publication Data
Heldring, Thatcher.
Toby Wheeler, eighth-grade benchwarmer / Thatcher Heldring. — 1st ed.
p. cm.
Summary: When Toby finally decides to join the middle school basketball team, he does not anticipate the changes that will occur in his relationship with his best friend JJ, who is the team's star player, as well as in other areas of his life.
ISBN 978-0-385-73390-8 (hc) — ISBN 978-0-385-90405-6 (glb)
[1. Basketball—Fiction. 2. Friendship—Fiction.
3. Interpersonal relations—Fiction.] I. Title.

PZ7.H3734To 2007
[Fic]—dc22
2006036824

The text of this book is set in 13-point Adobe Caslon.

Printed in the United States of America
10 9 8 7 6 5 4 3 2 1
First Edition

For Staci and Jack

TOBY WHEELER

Eighth-Grade Benchwarmer

· 1 ·

For as long I'd been playing basketball, all I'd ever wanted to be was a gym rat. I was just happy playing the game. All the other stuff—coaches, practices, and drills—got in the way. Take my best friend, JJ. When varsity basketball practices started Monday, his sorry butt would be stuck in the school gym five days a week until January, while I was living free, playing pickup ball at our local rec center. Sure, there were those nights when JJ would bring down the house with a game winner and I would get just a little jealous because I wasn't down there on the court with him. But that was how it had always been, and as far as I knew, that was how it would always be. I was the gym rat and he was the star.

How that all changed started around Halloween—which had a lot do with it, too. We were playing pickup ball with the gym rats. It was five on five and as always, we were playing to eleven, win by two, which meant the game continued until one team scored two straight baskets. If the teams traded baskets, like we had been doing for twenty minutes, there was no telling how long it would go on.

At the moment, I had two things on my mind. Trick-or-treating. And of course beating Vinny Pesto. Vinny was first. He was the captain of the basketball team at Hamilton Middle School—our school's archrival. Vinny and I had been going at it since the sixth grade. He never let me forget that Hamilton had won the league championship the year before. And I never let him forget that he was a cherry-picking ball-hog chump who wore his team jersey to open gym—major loser move.

I had just missed a jump shot and now Vinny was letting me hear about it, as usual. "That's a nice two-handed jump shot, Wheeler," he said. "They teach you that at Gym Rat Junior High?"

"That's a nice costume, Pesto," I shot back quickly. "I didn't know they sold dog-butt masks."

I used my jersey to wipe the sweat from my hands and smiled, thinking how Vinny was one of the best things and worst things about open gym. The worst because he *always* seemed to get me in the end. The best because without him, it wouldn't be any fun.

JJ was taking it easy that day, holding back. Every once in a while we'd try to run some no-look pass we'd practiced on the hoop on our street, but usually that led to a turnover. Otherwise JJ was just having fun and laughing at the dumb stuff Vinny and I were saying to each other. JJ moved without the ball, played defense, and passed off instead of shooting. But anyone who had seen him play knew he could switch his game on like a light.

In the meantime, it was the Toby vs. Vinny show. Vinny hit an ugly runner off the glass to put his team back up by one. I hit an eight-footer from the baseline. He scooped in a shot on a drive after taking more steps than a walkathon. I let it go, since this was pickup ball, and answered with a little magic of my own—a slash and dish to Old Dude for a layup. Vinny came back with his go-to move—the jab-step, pull-back jumper—and nailed it.

"I think we can beat these guys," I told JJ even though we were down by one and Vinny's team had the ball. There was no answer so I added, "What do you think—JJ?"

But JJ was focused on the doorway, where two men were watching us play. That was unusual. We didn't get many spectators at open gym. JJ's dad was on the right in heavy boots and a thick work jacket. The other man was larger than him—thick in the middle with a neck like an ox. He was dressed in nice pants and a sport coat. He had a tie, too, and glasses. They had been talking and pointing for a minute or so when JJ's dad whistled, gestured to the other man, and mouthed to JJ, *This is him.* He mimed a jump shot and nodded. Translation: Shoot.

JJ closed his eyes, exhaled, and opened them again, ready to play. One thing about JJ's dad—when he said shoot, you shot. First we had to get the rock back. I wondered who the other man was, but Vinny interrupted me before I could ask. "Ready to get burned like a piece of firewood, scrub?" he asked, bouncing me the ball so we could check it in.

I returned the ball. "Ready to get stuffed like a turkey, loser?"

Vinny passed, then got the ball back. He dribbled in place. It was a showdown. *You are not winning this one, Pesto.* I went into lockdown mode, keeping him between me and the basket, ready to pounce the second he twitched. "Stay with me, gym rat," he said. My eyes never left his. I knew his tics like the back of my hand. A quick breath meant he was going to drive. A curl of the lip meant he was going to shoot. *Gimme what you got, hotshot.* All of a sudden, the pace of his dribble quickened. He went from his left to his right hand and back to his left—*ba-dum, ba-dum, ba-dum.* On the last *ba-dum,* he inhaled and cut inside. I tried to stay with him, but crossed my own feet and stumbled. Vinny laughed all the way to the hoop, but shut his mouth when he got there. Like a lightning bolt, JJ had flashed across from the weak side as Vinny rose for the layup and snatched the ball cleanly away—almost in midair.

Vinny might have called foul, but JJ's dad whistled and clapped, causing play to stop while everyone looked around. We never got a lot of fans at the rec center. While I caught my breath and silently thanked JJ for coming alive at the right time, Old Dude shuffled past me. "Watch the ball, not the man," he said, winking. Old Dude was old—old enough to have a few gray hairs and two knee braces that made him look a bit like a robot in short shorts—but he knew his basketball.

JJ had the ball now, with Blue Shirt sticking him tight. Too bad for Blue Shirt—JJ was harder to guard than a ghost. One second JJ was standing in front of him with the ball. Just chilling on the right wing. Close enough to touch. Then he jab-stepped, pump-faked, and *poof,* he was on his way to the basket, and the game was tied. Blue Shirt just stood there, frozen, first staring straight ahead, then down at his blue shirt.

The game went on full speed now. Before we had a chance to get set on defense, Vinny's team inbounded the ball and rushed it upcourt. Blue Shirt wound up with it but was too strong on a shot that would have put them back up by one. I got the rebound and brought it back the other way. I raced up the right sideline, dribbling the ball with my outside hand. When I got to midcourt someone yelled "Whoooop," which in gym rat means "I'm open!" I looked up and a half second later felt the ball go off my toe and out of bounds. Turnover.

I could see JJ's dad slap his hat against his thigh. He wasn't pleased. But that changed the instant JJ jumped in front of the inbounds pass and flipped it behind his back to Old Dude. We were up by one! Then Blue Shirt saw Vinny cherry-picking and hurled a full-court bomb that hit the wall behind the hoop. Our ball! Now JJ's dad was crouching on the sideline, nearly pulling his hat apart.

Sport Coat was watching closely, too. You can tell sometimes by the look in someone's eye that he's taking notes in his head, and that was what this guy was doing—taking notes. But about what—or who? Me? It was bad enough I had just blown a chance to tie the game again. I didn't need strangers thinking about it too. I caught up to JJ near the free-throw line and asked him about the mystery man.

"That's him," JJ said, "our new coach. Well, my new coach."

"What's he doing here?" I asked.

"Dad brought him. It's his way of helping."

"Helping who?"

"Coach. Me. Himself. I don't know," JJ said quietly. When JJ turned on his game, he turned off something else. He disappeared into some autopilot mode. After that, he wasn't playing, he was working. It must have had something to do with his dad—or coach—because the moment he saw them was the moment he had stopped having fun.

To bring JJ back, I punched him in the shoulder. "Let's run Boardman," I said. Boardman was one of our plays. We named it after our street, where we made it up. Basically, all that happened was that one of us—usually JJ—started in the corner, cut to the wing, then to the baseline for a back-door pass.

JJ glanced at his dad, then at me again. He shook the hair from his face, knocked my fist with his, and said, "Game on."

Game on was our own greeting. It started on Boardman Street too. Whenever a car would come by, we'd say "Car" and stop the game. Then, when the car was gone, we'd yell "Game on!" and the game would continue. Before long, we began using it on the phone. Instead of "Hey, are we playing?" it would be "Game on?" After a while, "Game on" just took the place of "Hello" altogether.

JJ checked the ball in with his man. Vinny lined up against me in the corner. "This is it, Pesto," I said. "You're going down like Old Yeller."

Vinny tapped his captain patch. "I don't know who that is, but trust me, gym rat, even *with* your superstar friend, you will never, ever beat the greatest show on earth."

A moment later, we were running Boardman. I caught a laser-perfect pass from JJ on the baseline and sliced to the basket. Unfortunately, I sliced too far and ended up under the hoop. Leaning back, I tried to maneuver the ball in, but it clanked against the bottom of the rim. From the sideline, I heard the sound of a hat being slapped again. After that, things got sloppy. We turned it over twice more—once when Headband passed to the wrong guy, and once when my look-pass hit JJ in the back. A couple of jump shots and a layin later, the game was over and Vinny was standing at mid-court taunting the next challengers.

For the record, that was Vinny Pesto: 8,497,330. Toby Wheeler: 0.

After the game, JJ's dad pulled him aside, leaving me alone with the new coach. He offered his giant bear paw. "I'm Coach Applewhite," he said.

I shook his hand. "Toby Wheeler."

"That was a nice finish on the back-door cut, Toby. Why didn't I see your name on my roster?"

I had to admit, I was flattered. The coach of the basketball team had just complimented me. But it would take more than a little flattery to get *me* in uniform. I had heard a rumor that he had coached in college, and that his players would have to practice like college players. If I had avoided the team when Mr. Morales, the math teacher, was the coach, there was no way I was going within a million miles of that gym now that Sergeant College was in charge.

"I like it here, Coach," I said.

"Well, I could use someone like you. Just something to think about." Coach handed me a flyer. "If you change your mind, this is your ticket in."

"Thank you, sir," I said, taking the sheet of paper before Coach left the gym. "I'll think about it."

A few feet away, JJ and his dad were going at it. JJ's

dad wanted him to come straight home to look at game tapes from last season. Trying not to make a scene, JJ was pleading his case. "Can we do it some other time?" he said as I stood nearby, unsure whether to leave the rec center or keep waiting, which was getting uncomfortable.

The other gym rats were passing by. Some looked over. Others just hustled out the doors to the parking lot.

"Your season starts next week. What's so important you can't watch an hour of videotape? You might see something to give you an edge on the court."

"I'm going out," JJ said without offering any details.

But his dad pressed. "Where? With who?"

"With . . . Toby."

I knew JJ's dad thought I was okay. Mostly because when JJ and I were together, there was a pretty good chance we were playing basketball. "Well, I suppose that's all right then," he said, slipping on his beat-up hat. "I have some things to pick up in Everett anyway. But I'll be home in a couple of hours."

He followed us to the lobby, then went his own way. JJ seemed happy to see him go. And I was looking forward to a big night out.

· 2 ·

Outside, it was a bright blue afternoon—the first day of sunshine after a week of steady rain. All around the neighborhood, people were raking, cleaning gutters, and gathering fallen branches. That night would be cool, crisp, and clear: perfect trick-or-treating weather. JJ and I had gone out every Halloween since my family moved to Pilchuck from Seattle. When Dad got a job with the Landover Lumber Company, a small lumber company in Washington State, Mom grumbled a bit because she thought the lumber companies were to blame for everything, but she came around when she realized how close Pilchuck was to the mountains. That was five years earlier.

Today, fall was in the air, and I was enjoying the walk home with JJ. Outside in the breeze, the emotion from the game evaporated with the sweat. It was a feeling of accomplishment. I had played my butt off all afternoon. It would have been nice to beat Pesto, of course, but there would be other days.

To get back to our street from the rec center, we cut through the empty lot next to the ranger station and continued down Wentworth Street. JJ was quiet— nodding slowly to a beat in his head while he drummed a stick against fence posts, mailboxes, stop signs, and whatever else we passed. He wore his favorite green track jacket zipped to the top and baggy pants over duct-taped shoes. His hair was hanging loosely too, falling over his ears and into his eyes. It used to be buzzed short, like mine, but since summer he had let it grow long.

We came to the light at Verlot Street, where the logging trucks passed through town on their way to and from the mountains, leaving behind a permanent trail of wood chips and sawdust. Strung across the middle of Verlot Street was a sign that said in giant forest-green letters: BASKETBALL SEASON STARTS NOVEMBER 5TH. LET'S GO, CHUCKERS!

The same words were written across the top of the schedule I was clutching in my right hand—the piece of paper the new coach had handed me.

Then there were the signs that had nothing to do with basketball. They were tacked to telephone poles and taped to store windows. Some said SAVE THE SALMON, while others said SAVE OUR JOBS. These particular signs had appeared over the summer, when

Landover Lumber announced plans to harvest the south slope of Butte Peak, which we called Butt Peak because that was kind of how it was spelled—and how it looked. The town had seen a hundred fights like this and I figured we'd see a hundred more until either the trees were gone, the salmon were gone, or both.

JJ was still quiet as we turned off Verlot Street and made our way through a wooded area of mossy fir trees where we used to build forts out of stumps and fallen logs. Once we were on Boardman Street, I started plotting out our route for later. The houses on our block were smaller and much older than the newer houses on the edge of town. Most were built before I was born, when Pilchuck was just another logging town in the middle of nowhere. Back then, I guess, one house looked like every other. Over time, though, things changed. Some of the Pilchuckers who once made a living cutting down trees sold their homes to people who were moving up from the city. People like my parents, who bought the houses and fixed them up. But a few others, like JJ's family, stayed, and a lot of those houses never got backyard decks, paint jobs, or new kitchens.

When we were halfway down our street, I kicked through another pile of leaves and said, "I was thinking this year we should start on the edge of town and work our way in. If we start on our street, by the time we get out to the bigger houses, all the good stuff might be gone. Maybe my dad can drive us there so we don't lose any trick-or-treating time walking."

JJ tossed his stick away. "I'm not sure," he said.

"Okay, okay. We can walk. But we should hurry. It's three now. Sundown is five-oh-one. How soon can you get dressed?"

"Not about driving, Toby. About trick-or-treating."

That was when I saw Stephen coming up the street with Valerie. Stephen and Valerie had moved to Pilchuck over the summer while I was bird-watching on the Washington coast with my parents. Now Stephen and JJ had a band. Stephen had shaggy hair, wore an old green hat wherever he went, and was always high-fiving people. Valerie was his stepsister. I wasn't sure what JJ saw in her. She was always saying things she didn't mean, like "nice pants." From what I could tell, her only other friend was a pocket mirror.

"Hi," Valerie said.

"What's up?" JJ said.

We stood in a circle near the curb. A witch and a ballerina passed by, lugging bags of candy. Nobody said anything. I watched Valerie shiver, then inch closer to JJ. *Is this what he does with Stephen and Valerie? Stand around and look at each other? Boring.* To pass the time, I began bouncing the basketball off the vertical pole in front of me. I made five in a row. Then ten in a row.

I was on twelve when Stephen pulled a drumstick from his back pocket and said, "So, are we on?"

Let him down easy, JJ, I thought.

But JJ said, "Let's do it, man."

Whoa! Personal foul! What happened to trick-or-treating?

My hands slipped as the ball flew forward.

The ball sailed past the pole and collided with Valerie's forehead.

"*Ow!*" she shrieked, falling to the ground.

"Sorry," I said, watching anxiously as JJ helped her up. That was worse than usual. Normally, around girls, I just stuttered, turned red, and ran for my life.

"So do you guys want to come inside?" JJ asked Valerie, obviously hoping to move past the incident.

I was running out of time! "Aren't you forgetting something?" I asked.

"Um, no. I don't think so," JJ said.

Valerie said, "JJ, what is he talking about?"

Ignoring her, I turned to JJ. "You know . . ." I held my hands out like I was holding a bag. "Ding-dong."

They stared at me. Man, did I have to spell it out for these people?

"Ding-dong," I repeated. I waved my hands around. "*OOOHHOOOO.*"

This was getting awkward.

"*Trick-or-treat?*" I whispered.

"Wait," said Valerie, rubbing her forehead and putting it together, "you want to go *trick-or-treating?*"

"Is there something wrong with that?" I asked. "JJ, you want to go too, right? You just told your dad you were coming out with me." Of course, JJ had not told his dad he was going *trick-or-treating* with me—he'd just told him he was going out. It hit me like the basketball had hit Valerie. JJ was embarrassed to go trick-or-treating. I could see it in the way he was looking at his shoes. He didn't want to face his new friends.

Stephen spoke next. "Valerie, why do you have to talk like that to people? If Toby wants to go, he should go."

"I was just *clarifying* that he wanted to go trick-or-treating. I wasn't judging, *Stephen*. Why do you always have to stand up for people?"

"Maybe because you're always putting them down."

"That's just my voice. I can't help it." Valerie flipped her head around to face me. "Have fun trick-or-treating, Toby," she said. "I think it's great you still want to do that stuff."

As Valerie took JJ's hand to lead him away, he turned and said, "Sorry, man. I wish I could."

"Save us some candy," Stephen added.

"So, is that a no?" I called to their backs.

Down the street, Valerie laughed at something JJ said.

"Call me if you change your mind!" I shouted.

But they were gone.

Watching them disappear up the street, I felt very small. All around me now were ghosts and witches—all of them much shorter than me. Was that how JJ and his friends saw me? As a little ghost who still wanted to dress up on Halloween? Well, so what if I did? I bet part of JJ wanted the same thing, even if he was too ashamed to admit it.

The wind picked up, blowing cold air down from the mountains. I stuck my hands in my pockets. The crumpled-up schedule was there. I pulled it out and looked it over. Ten games. Two months of practices. Every one of those nights and days was another hour when JJ would be doing something else without me— and now his free time was all about the band, and the girl. Shaggy and Snotty. What could I do about it? I didn't play an instrument. I didn't know the first thing about girls. All I had was basketball.

· 3 ·

When I came into the kitchen, Dad was fixing a tinfoil axe head to a broom handle. He was wearing a red flannel shirt, wool pants with suspenders, and work boots. Across the room, Mom was standing with her arms crossed. She had antlers. Her nose was painted brown.

"Nice costume, Dad," I said. "Where's your ox?"

"I don't have an ox tonight," he said. "Just a grouchy deer."

Mom smiled at me, adjusted her antlers, and said to Dad, "I just don't see why you have to wear *that* costume every year."

"I do work for a lumber company, Maureen." It was true. Except Dad didn't cut down trees. Dad's job was to sell the wood chips left on the mill floor to home improvement stores, where people bought them for garden mulch and playgrounds. When he and Mom agreed to leave Seattle, part of the reason was that Dad thought he had a bright future with Landover Lumber. Dad was kind of a dreamer, but I didn't think selling wood chips was the stuff of his dreams.

Dad stomped over to the middle of the room and leaned his giant axe against the island. "What do you have against Paul Bunyan, Maureen?" he asked.

"Paul Bunyan is a symbol of reckless deforestation," Mom said as the doorbell rang. Before she left the kitchen to hand out candy, she added, "I don't think we should be celebrating the destruction of natural habitats."

Mom wasn't just talking. She worked at this place called the Cascade Group. When you lived where we did, there was always some marsh or stretch of woods about to be cut for lumber or to make room for a housing development. The Cascade Group was supposed to protect those areas by making a lot of noise in the newspapers and on television. Right now, Mom was fighting to save the south slope of Butte Peak from being harvested by Landover Lumber. It had something to do with salmon. I wouldn't want to be Landover Lumber with Maureen Wheeler on the case. Mom's really the competitive one in the family, even if it has nothing to do with sports.

"Destruction of natural habitats," Dad muttered when we were alone in the kitchen. Then he snapped his suspenders and said to me, "I don't care what she says. I think I look great." He clapped his hands excitedly. "Did I tell you Warren Goodman at work recommended me for a promotion?"

I looked Dad in the eye. It wasn't hard. He was barely taller than me, meaning he had about a half inch on the average eighth grader. He wasn't carrying much in the middle, either. His belt was cinched in to the last hole. If a tree had fallen in the woods and Dad had been standing nearby, I think the breeze would have blown him over.

"What kind of promotion?"

"In the main office, Toby. Working with the big boys. No more wood chips." Dad pulled a soda out of the refrigerator. When the can was open, he caught his reflection in the mirror. He stood there for a moment admiring the image before looking at me. "No costume for you tonight?" he said.

"No," I sighed.

Dad sat at the kitchen table. "You're not going out with JJ?"

"He's with his *other* friends," I said, sitting opposite Dad as Mom came back from the front door. We were all at the kitchen table now—the gym rat, the deer, and Paul Bunyan. "He said he thinks we're too old to trick-or-treat. Can you believe that? All of a sudden he just decides he doesn't want to do it anymore. He'd rather play his guitar and stand around doing nothing with Valerie. How can that be more fun than trick-or-treating?" I tore open a candy bar. "It's all their fault."

"Whose fault?" Dad asked.

"Valerie and Stephen. If they hadn't come along, JJ would be out there with me, just like every other year."

Dad squeezed my shoulder. "If you're not spending as much time with JJ as you used to, maybe you should find something you both like to do."

"Like what?"

"You can work at the mill," said Dad. "We'll pay you to bag wood chips after school. You can do it together."

"JJ has basketball after school," I said.

Dad tried again. "Then why don't you join the basketball team?"

"I met the new coach today," I told them. "He said I could come to practice on Monday."

"What did you say?" Mom asked.

"That I would think about it."

Dad was quiet for a while. "You know, I never played on sports teams when I was in school," he said. "I always felt I was missing out on something. The football team seemed like an army unit to me. It made me jealous. You just don't find that kind of camaraderie in the Latin club."

"I play sports, Dad. Just not on the team."

"There's a difference, Toby," he replied. "I'm not sure you're really giving yourself a chance to be what you can be by avoiding real basketball."

That made my neck burn. "Pickup ball *is* real basketball. We play with ten guys, two hoops, and one ball.

Just because we don't wear uniforms or have a coach doesn't mean it's not basketball."

Mom stared me down. "Don't speak like that to your father," she said. "He has a good point. If you want to spend more time with JJ and you want to prove yourself as a basketball player, then you have no reason not to give the team a shot."

"You didn't even want the school to hire a basketball coach," I said. Coach Applewhite was the first full-time basketball coach Pilchuck had ever had. Before him, a teacher or parent had always run the team. After a string of losing seasons, though, the school board had decided enough was enough. I thought it was great, but some people, like Mom, thought the town had better things to spend its money on—like saving the south slope of Butte Peak.

Mom popped an M&M into her mouth. "Well, now that we've got one, we might as well use him."

That night I lay awake in bed. I was thinking about what Dad had said about missing out on something. I didn't know exactly what he meant, but from the look in his eye, there was no doubt he was telling me something real. I remembered a night less than a year before. It was a home game. JJ hit the winning shot at the buzzer. The crowd went wild, of course. But what stuck with me was watching his eleven teammates carry him off to the locker room, while I stood halfway up the bleachers, wondering what it would feel like to be one of those twelve. JJ and I were best friends. It should have been my arm around him after that game. If we were on the same team, maybe he would see me as an equal, and not as his friend from across the street who still wanted to go trick-or-treating. By the time I faded to sleep, I was still confused. It was the next day, at the rec center, when Vinny Pesto cleared everything up.

· 4 ·

It wasn't the first time I had ever seen a girl at the rec center, but it was the first time I had ever seen *her*. She said her name was Megan. She had long brown hair; a lean, freckled face; and skinny arms. She wore a light blue T-shirt and baggy red shorts, and whenever she shot, she glared at the ball while it was in midair like she was daring it not to go in, which it usually did. Although we had been on the same team all afternoon, "Good game" and "Nice shot" were all we had said.

After three hours of full-court five-on-five, everyone was breathing hard. Sweat hung in the air like storm clouds. It was so humid inside the rec center, the tagboard signs advertising KARATE! and AEROBICS! were peeling off the brick walls. One was hanging by a single corner.

At the moment, I had the ball at the top of the arc.

The game was tied 9–9. I dribbled in place and considered my options. On my right was Goggles. As usual, Goggles was calling for the ball even though he was guarded. I looked inside. Old Dude and Blue Shirt were setting screens for each other on the baseline.

Megan was playing on the perimeter with me. She had a smooth motion and a high-arcing jump shot that floated through the net. On this possession, though, I wanted the ball. I wanted to take it myself. After all, standing between me and the hoop was Vinny Pesto. Ball in hand, I stared him down, hoping to psych him out. Fat chance. Vinny glared back at me. He raised one arm, bent his knees, and tapped his chest.

"You should save your energy and give me the ball now, gym rat."

"You can't stop me, Pesto," I said, showing him a crossover.

Vinny swiped at the ball. "Bring it on."

Switching the ball from my right hand to my weaker left hand, I drove. Backpedaling, Vinny kept between me and the basket. When I was within six feet of the hoop, I went airborne. I figured I would either get off a shot or dump the ball off to Old Dude for a layin. But as soon as I left the floor, the lane was clogged with bodies, leaving me no room to shoot and nowhere to pass. The ball squirted free. Vinny grabbed it, ran the other way, and laid it in, giving his team the lead, 10–9.

If there was an award for cherry-picking, Vinny Pesto would win the trophy every year.

Old Dude came up to me at midcourt. "Don't ever leave your feet without a plan," he said, adjusting one of his knee braces.

"Thanks," I said. "I usually make that."

Vinny checked the ball to me. I called out the score and passed the ball in to Goggles, who instantly shot. Miraculously, the ball rattled in and we were tied again.

10–10.

Scowling, Vinny took the inbounds pass and set up the offense. He had a man wide open under the basket—the guy Goggles was supposed to be guarding. But Goggles was cherry-picking under the other basket. Sure enough, Vinny ignored the open man and, with my hand in his face, fired a jump shot from eighteen feet. The ball fell off the rim and into Old Dude's hands. Old Dude airmailed a pass to Goggles, who caught the ball, missed, gathered his own rebound, and put it up again. This time, the ball fell through the net.

11–10.

Then Vinny's big man turned the ball over, dribbling upcourt.

I've been there, Big Man.

It was our ball. I nodded at Megan.

She nodded back. *Let's get it done.*

Then I looked at Vinny. "One more and it's over, Pesto." There was no way he was wriggling off the hook this time.

Vinny smiled. I had to give him credit. He was sweating, but he was cool. "Hey, gym rat," he said, "where's your so-called friend? Did he ditch you for the basketball team again?"

"He couldn't make it today," I shot back, hoping nobody could see Vinny was getting to me. "He's got a date with your sister."

But Vinny brushed the comeback aside. He smelled blood. "If he was really your friend," he taunted, "he'd be here now. Not off with his *real* teammates."

I was choking the basketball. My teeth were grinding. "You don't know what you're talking about, Pesto."

That was when Vinny went for the kill.

"Why don't you just face it, gym rat?" he said, letting the words hang in the air. "JJ's too good for you."

That did it. I hurled the ball at Vinny's feet. He timed his jump well and it bounced away. My fists clenched. We were nose to nose now. Too close to punch—lucky for him. "For your information, chump, JJ is *not* too good for me. And I could play on that team anytime I wanted to. I have a personal invitation from the coach."

That seemed to surprise Megan. Her eyebrows went up.

Vinny tilted his head back and stepped out of range. "Then why don't you?" he said.

He meant play on the team.

"Maybe I will," I said, surprising myself.

"What?" Vinny laughed as though he hadn't heard me right. "You?"

"Yeah, me," I said. "Is that funny?"

"It's more than funny," he said. "It's impossible! You're a *gym rat*. You don't know the first thing about real basketball. You probably think a pick-and-roll comes with butter." Vinny paused. Everyone was watching, and he was really enjoying it. He made a big deal out of scratching his head. "On the other hand," he said as my fingers dug into my palms and my forehead burned like an iron, "we are talking about Pil-suck, so maybe you do belong on the team. Maybe this is the year you and the other Pil-chumps finally get out of the basement."

"Just wait, Vinny. We're not gonna be anywhere near the basement. As a matter of fact, we're gonna be in the championship game."

"Oh yeah?"

"Yeah. And *I'm* gonna hit the winning shot."

"In your dreams, gym rat."

"Not in my dreams, Pesto. In your face."

That was when Megan pulled me aside.

"That's right, gym rat," Vinny called. "Talk it over with Mrs. Gym Rat."

We walked a few steps away. Well, Megan walked. I bounced backward, ready to swat back anything else Vinny had to send my way.

I was still fired up. "That's the last time Vinny Pesto tells me a gym rat can't play *real* basketball."

"Yeah," Megan said, drawing out her words, "you really showed him."

"What's that supposed to mean?"

"Toby, do you realize what you've done?"

"I scored one for all the gym rats, that's what I did."

"No, you just joined the basketball team. That's what you did."

"Good. Bring it on. I'll show *everyone* what real basketball is."

"Toby," Megan started to say, "there's something you should know—"

"I know what's coming for Vinny," I said.

Megan rolled her eyes. "Okay, you're right. One thing at a time. First, you know he'd do anything to stop *you* from beating him."

"Is that supposed to be good news?"

"It means if you set a screen for me, he won't switch. He'd rather leave me open than risk letting you out of his sight for a second. Trust me."

"So what do I do?"

I listened as Megan used her palm and fingers to draw up the play.

A moment later, I was checking the ball with Vinny.

It happened almost exactly like Megan said it would. I passed the ball in to her, then set a screen on her defender. She dribbled around me, leaving her man stuck behind the screen. And Vinny, instead of switching to guard Megan, stayed on me. Curling off the screen, Megan pulled up at the elbow, the spot on the court where the free-throw line meets the side of the key. Suddenly, the man guarding Blue Shirt rushed toward her, his long arms raised high. Megan never blinked.

She lifted a soft jumper over the outstretched arm of the charging defender. The shot went up like a rainbow, then splashed down through the net.

12–10.

I threw my arms up in the air like we had just won a championship. Maybe it was a little over the top, but at that moment I was going a hundred miles an hour on pure emotion. Not far off, Vinny was barking at his teammates for not playing defense. When he saw me, he said, "Don't get a big head over this, gym rat. You still needed someone else to win the game for you."

"Pilchuck plays Hamilton in three weeks, Pesto. And I'll be there."

"I'll be sure to wave to you on the bench, scrub."

But nothing Vinny could say would dampen my mood that day. I had won. It was now Vinny Pesto: 8,497,330; Toby Wheeler: 1.

· 5 ·

Twenty minutes later, Megan and I were standing on the corner where Verlot Street begins. We'd stuck around the rec center after open gym, reliving the game, until the assistant director, Alberto, kicked us out so he could mop the floors before the aerobics ladies came in with their mats. Outside in the damp breeze, Megan had suggested we go for pizza.

I told her I never said no to pizza.

Usually, when I walked home from the rec center, I forgot all about the action on the court. But that day was different; tomorrow, I was going to show the world that a gym rat could play team ball, and that no matter what Vinny Pesto said, JJ was not too good for me. I was going to be JJ's *real* teammate just like the rest of those suckers. The way I figured, they had never seen anything like Toby Wheeler.

Corner Pizza was empty except for a couple of men playing pool. The restaurant was dimly lit, with peeling walls and wood booths that people had been carving their names into for centuries. To avoid the cold air from outside, we chose a booth in the back, across from the arcade games. JJ and I used to have a running competition on the Hoop Shoot. The standing record was twenty-four shots in sixty seconds. I set that on the last day of seventh grade, the last time we'd played.

Megan smiled from across the booth, then frowned as if she had remembered something important. "I have to call home," she said. As she was dialing, she turned to me and quickly whispered, "It might be better if you don't say anything while I'm talking. Technically, I'm not supposed to be doing this."

While Megan was on the phone, I looked around, trying to figure out what it was she wasn't supposed to be doing. Eating pizza on a school night?

"I'm just getting pizza, Dad," Megan was saying. "With who? Who am I getting pizza with?" Megan held the phone away from her mouth, bit her lower lip, then said casually, "Um, a girl I met . . . playing basketball at the rec center. . . . Yeah, she's pretty good. . . . A little raw. . . . Okay, I will. . . . I *know*, Dad. No boys." Now Megan was pretending to pull out her hair. Finally she said, "Tell Mom I don't need dinner. I'll be home by dark," and hung up.

Megan tossed her phone into her gym bag. "Sorry about that. My dad is a little paranoid."

As long as we never met face to face in a dark alley, he could be as paranoid as he wanted to be. "Hey, my dad sells *wood chips* for a living," I said. "Nobody's perfect." Still, I hoped Megan was exaggerating. Nobody wanted a deranged father chasing him around town. "What does your dad do?" I asked.

Megan tore the paper off her straw. "He coaches basketball. . . ."

Gulp.

"That's what I was trying to tell you," she continued. "My dad is going to be your coach. Well, that was part of it." Megan shed her raincoat and hung it on the end of the booth. "Do you still want to join the team?" she asked.

"I thought I did."

"You have nothing to worry about. He'll never know I was with you. And even if he did, he'd have to go through me first."

After we ordered, Megan told me more. A lot more. For instance, starting the next day, she was going to be a new student at my school.

"Why did you move to Pilchuck?" I asked.

As Megan took a long sip of her Coke, I tried to look at her without staring. Her hair was still pulled back, and there was a smudge on her cheek, maybe where someone had bumped into her during open gym. When she blinked, I noticed for the first time that her eyes were blue. Suddenly there was a crack from the pool table. One of the men, a giant with hands like catcher's mitts, cursed and handed the stick to the other man. I thought about Megan's paranoid dad and remembered seeing him in the gym the day before. He had seemed big enough to bend steel. That was when I got a little paranoid myself. I would be crazy to join the team now. What would he do to me if he knew I was the one who took his daughter out for pizza? He'd use me as an example, that was what. Like island tribes who stick the shrunken heads of their victims on posts to warn away trespassers.

"Two years ago," she said, "my dad was coaching a small college in Portland. He was working *all* the time, sleeping in his office, eating fast food twenty-four/seven. If he wasn't getting ready for a game, he was on the road, recruiting at high schools and jucos."

"Jucos?" I asked as the waiter delivered our pizza.

"Junior colleges," Megan explained. "Anyway, if he won a game, he'd come home all smiles and my mom and I would see him for about a day. But even then, we had to snap to get him to answer a question."

"Slice?" I asked Megan, balancing a steaming piece of pepperoni.

"Thanks," Megan said, holding out her plate. She continued, "But if he lost a game, he went back to the office. With him it was basketball, basketball, basketball."

"So what happened?"

Megan let her slice cool. "The past season, his team was supposed to compete for a conference title. But they had some injuries and some bad games. By the end of the season, they were in last place. And Dad was worn out. He went to the doctor, who told him he needed to take it easy and watch his blood pressure. So he quit his job and came home." Megan took a bite of her pizza, wiped her hands with a napkin, and went on. "At first it was good. He was rested and healthy again. Then he got bored and started watching talk shows all day because his doctor wouldn't let him watch basketball. I think that's when he came up with the 'no boys' rule. He watched this show called Dr. Barb. After that, every time I wanted to go somewhere, he would tell me about some girl on Dr. Barb who went to the mall and ended up getting kidnapped. Luckily, a friend told him Pilchuck was hiring a basketball coach. I didn't really want to leave, but at least it got Dad out of the house again. And Mom thought coaching middle school would be a way to do what he loves, but with less pressure than college. So we moved."

"Do you miss your old school?"

Megan thought about it for a minute. "So much," she said finally. I thought she was going to say more, but it sounded like the rest of the words were caught in her throat. Instead, she shook it off and added, "I can't believe I'm telling you all this. I don't even know you. You must think I'm nuts."

I didn't think she was nuts. I thought she was the first girl I could talk to without passing out. And even though I was already sort of scared of her dad, I had to know what had happened to him. "Your dad is fine now, right?"

"He has to monitor his blood pressure. Too much excitement or stress could get him in trouble."

"Maybe he won't take things so seriously this time," I said.

Through a mouthful of pizza Megan replied, "You don't know my dad."

When we were finished, we left Corner Pizza. I walked Megan to the light. It was drizzling, so she pulled up her hood and tightened the drawstrings. "Does it snow much here?" she asked.

"It snows a lot," I said. "And it gets cold. Last year we had an early freeze and there was a rush on wood chips so everyone could cover their plants before winter. Dad was working late every night filling orders."

Megan nodded politely, but she must have been wondering why I was going on and on about wood chips. So I cut myself off and said, "Well, thanks again for helping me beat Pesto."

"Thanks for being nice to the new girl."

"No problem. I guess I'll see you around school."

I had taken three steps when Megan called, "Toby?"

"Yeah."

"Tomorrow, at practice," she said. "Be ready to run."

On the way home, I sent JJ a text message: I'm coming to practice tomorrow.

Later that night I got a message back: It won't be like the rec center.

· 6 ·

My brain was running out of oxygen. Thoughts were coming slowly. All around me, guys were bent over clutching the bottom of their shorts, gasping for breath, dreading the whistle. My legs seemed ready to buckle any minute. How had I gotten myself into this?

I showed up for the first practice, that was how.

I looked up at the clock and prayed for four-thirty when practice was *supposed* to end. At least that was what Roy Morelli had promised me an hour earlier. We had been running nonstop since then. We hadn't even touched a basketball! Back and forth, across the width of the gym we ran, again and again, until my sides ached and my lungs burned like coals.

Finally, at four-fifteen, Coach Applewhite brought

out a basketball. *That's more like it,* I thought. *Who's up for some five-on-five?* Just the idea of playing an actual game revived me. This was my chance to show them what I could do.

Coach stood on the baseline and sized us up. His shirt was pressed free of wrinkles and tucked neatly into his slacks. His shoes were spotless too—polished enough to reflect light from the ceiling. When he walked, his hair stayed frozen in place—like each strand was afraid to defy the man who combed it. Add to all that a pair of wire-frame glasses, and nobody would ever guess he was a coach and not a regular teacher—or even the principal.

Coach held up the basketball. "Who wants it?" His voice was low and commanding.

Nobody moved. Figuring Coach wanted a captain to pick teams, I said, "I'll do it."

Coach looked surprised. "Wheeler. Be my guest."

I stepped to the free-throw line. "I'll take JJ."

Embarrassed, JJ lowered his head.

The rest of the team laughed quietly.

Coach cleared his throat. "You'll take JJ where?"

"Aren't we choosing teams?"

More laughter from the baseline.

"Son, does this look like recess to you? This is how we finish practice. You shoot two free throws. If you make them both, we're done. If you miss one, we run. If you miss two, we run a little more."

I took a deep breath. It wasn't as though I had never made a free throw before. You just bent the knees, aimed, and shot. So I did. My shot went up. It was straight. There was hope. Maybe I would be the hero after all. Then the ball dropped from the sky like a wounded duck, falling a foot short of the rim. Air ball.

"Oh, man," Roy said. "Why did we let the rookie shoot the free throw?"

"Man, I wish the other benchwarmer hadn't quit after tryouts," said Khalil. "At least he could make a free throw."

The other benchwarmer? Why was Khalil comparing me to some benchwarmer? I guess he didn't know Coach had *asked* me to come to practice.

"We're gonna be here all day," someone added.

I glanced at JJ, thinking he might get them off my back. But he was looking away. Suddenly, I felt like I was in battle. I was under attack and cut off from my backup. I had never had so many people mad at me at once.

When we were done with the next set of sprints, Coach waved me back to the line. I shot again. This time the ball hit the front of the rim and rolled in.

"It's a miracle," said Roy.

"What would be a miracle, Morelli," Coach said to Roy, "is if you could keep your mouth shut long enough to make a free throw yourself."

Roy trudged to the free-throw line and wasted no time missing his first shot. Running on fumes, we wheezed through another set of sprints. I stumbled across the baseline at 4:31, dizzy with exhaustion and thankful to be alive. I collapsed on the bench and found a bottle of water in my bag. I stretched my legs out. It was so nice to lie down. Looking up, I was surprised to see that the rest of the team was still standing on the baseline, most of them holding their sides and breathing hard. Maybe they were cooling down, or just hanging out. Their choice. I closed my eyes and congratulated myself on surviving the first practice. When my eyes opened, Coach's face was nose to nose with mine.

"Wheeler, what in the world do you think you're doing?"

"Just having a drink, sir."

"Practice isn't over."

"But it's past—"

"Past what, Wheeler? Past your bedtime?"

Still more laughter from the baseline.

"Sorry, sir."

Coach's mouth was turned down at the corners. He did not look as impressed as he had the other day at the rec center. I was beginning to think I had mis-understood his *invitation*. He handed me the ball. "Two more."

Everyone groaned, including me. I didn't want me on the line any more than they wanted me on the line!

"I guarantee you there will be a game this season that comes down to a free throw," Coach said as my first shot tickled the twine. "The more comfortable you are making that shot in a pressure situation, the better. But it is even more important that all twelve of you be in shape. Conditioning wins championships, boys. Lesson number one for today. We don't play basketball to get in shape. We get in shape to play basketball." My second shot missed. He continued speaking as we ran. "We have ten games this season, not including playoffs, and I believe this team has a chance to win every single one of them if we work hard and play as a team."

I had to push myself to get through the wind sprints, but I wasn't the last one across the line. Raj led the way, with JJ, Roy, and Ruben darting on his heels. I was in the middle of the pack, huffing and puffing with Malcolm and McKlusky. Last place by a mile was Khalil, who chugged through his first lap but was wheezing badly when I looked back from the baseline. He was walking, too tired even to complain. That was when Ruben jogged over to him and guided him to the finish.

"Thanks, man," Khalil gasped. "I thought I wasn't going to make it."

I felt bad for Khalil, but I was also relieved that someone was slower than me.

Coach cleared his throat. "I know I'm new here, but I want you to know I already see a lot of potential in this team. I want you to be winners," he added, "not just for the sake of winning, but to experience what goes into winning: twelve individuals being a part of something bigger than any one person. Remember that: It takes twelve of you to win one game."

Coach Applewhite let that sink in while he brought a mesh bag to the center of the gym. Inside the mesh bag were jerseys. Some green, some white, and some red. "These are your practice jerseys," Coach explained. "First team wears green. Second team wears white. And there are two red jerseys for the reserves. I know we just started practicing, but I think it's important for every-body to have a role on the team from the beginning."

I felt a little sorry for whoever was going to wind up with a red shirt. But it was like Coach said, this was about more than any one person. I was pretty sure there was a white shirt in that bag for me. I didn't think Coach would make me a starter right away, so second team made the most sense. After all, he had seen me at the rec center.

There was no surprise when the first three green jer-seys went to JJ, Ruben, and Raj. The fourth green jersey went to Khalil and the fifth went to Roy, who played my position, shooting guard. McKlusky got the first white jersey. I sat up straight, waiting for Coach to call my name. The green team was huddled together, except for JJ, who stood apart like he was waiting for me to join him. But one after another, the white jerseys disap-peared, until there were none left. This was not the way it was supposed to go. No way had I given up my life at the rec center to be a reserve on the basketball team. To sit at the end of the bench, watching JJ from the sideline like nothing had ever changed. No way. This was what was going through my head as Coach Applewhite handed the first red jersey to the seventh grader, Malcolm, then said, "And last but not least, Toby Wheeler."

· 7 ·

The next day in math class, Mr. Morales introduced a unit on geometry. Standing in front of the classroom in a tie, with his shirtsleeves rolled up to his elbows, he explained the Pythagorean theorem. "If you know the lengths of two sides of a right triangle," he said in a way that made me think he thought he had discovered the formula himself, "you can calculate the length of the third side with a simple equation."

But my mind was not on triangles or rectangles or any angles at all. I had a problem, and no theorem was going to help me solve it. In one weekend, I had gone from a happy gym rat to the twelfth man on the basketball team. Sure, it was good to be on the team with JJ, and I was looking forward to road trips and stuff like that. But when was I going to *play*?

There was Vinny to worry about too. I had to work

fast. Our third game of the season was against Hamilton. If Pesto saw me on the end of the bench, he would never let me hear the end of it. I might have to fake an injury.

The bell rang and everyone packed their bags and filed toward the door. Mr. Morales stopped me as I passed his desk. "Toby, hang out for a second. I want to ask you something."

"I swear that sink was clogged when I went into the bathroom."

"Not that. I want to ask you a favor. I have a new student in my prealgebra class. She just started yesterday and she needs a little help getting caught up with the material. Since you were one of my best algebra students, I thought perhaps you could be her tutor. Just for a couple of weeks."

"Sure, Mr. Morales. I'll help."

Mr. Morales smiled as the door opened. "Here she is now. Toby, meet Megan Applewhite. Megan, this is Toby Wheeler, your math tutor."

Holding her bag close to her chest and hovering cautiously on the edge of the classroom, Megan said, "We've met."

I did a double take. What happened to the girl who set up the winning shot to beat Vinny Pesto? Or the girl with pizza sauce on her face at Corner Pizza? On Saturday her hair had been pulled back in a ponytail, and her gym shorts were covered in sweat. Today, her hair was parted straight down the middle and fell to her shoulders. Instead of a blue cotton T-shirt, she wore a button-down dress shirt, a dark skirt, and high-heel shoes. She still had the same blue eyes and freckles, though.

Because we were late, Mr. Morales gave us hall passes. As we were leaving the classroom, Megan looked down at her schedule, then up, then down, then up again. Finally she looked at me and asked, "Do you know where room two-twelve A is, Toby? This school is so big. I'm still getting used to it."

"Follow me," I said.

The bell had rung, so the hallway was empty. We walked quietly, the only sound the *click-clack* of Megan's shoes. We had reached the corner when we heard footsteps. Coming around the bend were JJ and Valerie.

JJ was startled but seemed relieved not to be facing a teacher. Still, he dropped Valerie's hand and retreated a half step toward a locker. "Toby. What are you doing here?" he said.

We have hall passes, I thought. *What are* you *doing here?*

I didn't want to be nosy, though, so instead I said, "I'm showing Megan where room two-twelve A is." That made me think of the class next door so I turned to Megan and added, "In sixth grade, JJ and I had music in room two-fourteen A, but we spent a lot of time out in the hallway—especially during rehearsals for the holiday recital. I was supposed to sing 'Walking in a Winter Wonderland' for my solo, only JJ gave me two candy canes to change the words to 'walking in a woman's underwear.' From then on, every time we sang 'Winter Wonderland,' we started laughing so hard Mrs. Morrison would just point to the door without saying anything. Oh, man, it was the best. Remember, JJ?"

JJ twisted a beat-up songbook in his hands. He had no backpack or any other books. Obviously he and Valerie were not on their way to class. Glancing down the empty hallway, he said, "Yeah, Toby. I remember. That was pretty funny."

Valerie smiled at Megan. "Are you new?"

"I just moved here," Megan said.

"I like your skirt," Valerie said.

"Thanks. What happened to your forehead?"

Remind me to thank Megan for *that* later.

Soon Megan and Valerie were speed-talking. Their voices had reached a pitch my ears could no longer detect. JJ had tuned out too. He was absentmindedly tapping the songbook against a locker, while I began twirling my elastic key chain around my pointer finger.

When Valerie gasped at the sound of a door closing, it was very startling. So startling that the key chain spun right off my finger and into Valerie's cheek. It fell to the floor with a *plink,* but not before leaving a red mark underneath Valerie's right eye. "Yeow!" she yelled. "Toby!"

The footsteps, which had been fading, stopped, then grew louder.

Valerie scooped up the key chain and threw it back at me. She missed and the keys rattled against a locker.

That was the moment Coach Applewhite rounded the corner and zeroed in on us like a heat-seeking missile. Megan and I were in the clear. We had hall passes. But JJ and Valerie were busted.

"What's going on here?" Coach asked, straightening his tie. "Megan, why aren't you in class?"

"Relax, Dad. We have hall passes."

"Megan," Coach said sternly. "Not in school."

"Sorry, Dad."

When Valerie heard Megan call Coach Applewhite *dad*, she popped her head to the side. "No *way*."

Coach peered at Valerie through his glasses. "Who's this?" he asked.

"This is Valerie, my friend."

Facing Valerie with his back to Megan, Coach asked, "Are you the one Megan had pizza with Sunday night?"

Megan nodded rapidly in Valerie's direction and mouthed, *Say yes.*

Valerie never missed a beat. "Yup, that was me, Coach Applewhite."

"And why aren't you in class?"

"Sh-she was showing me where room two-twelve A was," Megan sputtered.

Would Coach buy it? We held our breath. Slowly, he looked us all over once more, told everyone to go straight to class, then turned on his heel and marched away.

"*Phew*," said Megan and Valerie at the same time. This caused them both to laugh hysterically. JJ and I looked at each other and shrugged. When the coast was clear, he and Valerie darted off down the hallway, then out the side door that led to the wooded area behind the school. I dropped Megan off at room 212A for earth science, then hustled around the corner to social studies. One thing bothered me. Megan had said the other night that I had nothing to worry about when it came to her father. But why then did she turn sheet-white and panic when Coach asked Valerie if she was the person Megan had been with on Sunday? If Megan had a reason to be nervous about her dad, didn't I?

· 8 ·

By Thursday, I had realized one thing: When it came to basketball practice, being the twelfth man was no picnic. I had to show up on time every day and run wind sprints whenever someone missed a layin or a free throw or whenever Coach Applewhite felt like blowing his whistle. Then I stood on the sideline while Coach walked the first and second teams through the offense. Once in a while it was fun. Sometimes, if one of the players wasn't catching on, Coach would take the guy by the arm and act like he was helping a blind man across the street, which usually got a laugh. But that just led to more wind sprints and Coach lecturing us that if we were laughing in practice, we weren't taking it seriously, and if we weren't taking it seriously, we shouldn't be there at all. I stuck it out, looking forward to the moment JJ and I would be on the court together. In the meantime, my way of taking practice seriously was to *try* to listen to Coach, while the other odd man out, Malcolm, made comments like this:

"That's not what Malcolm would have done."

"Malcolm would've dunked that."

"You're lucky Malcolm isn't guarding you."

"Coach better get Malcolm the ball soon, baby."

Coach had spent most of those first three days teaching us the offense—a motion offense. The idea was to move without the ball and set screens for each other to get the best shot possible. Raj always brought the ball upcourt. Khalil and Ruben were the post players. They set up on one side. Roy started on the wing, above Khalil and Roy, isolating JJ on the other wing. Coach insisted JJ get an open look on every offensive possession. The fact that Coach was running the offense through JJ made me feel like a million dollars because, to me, JJ was just the guy I had shot hoops with a thousand times on Boardman Street, and if I could play with him there, I figured I could play with anyone, anywhere. Coach also told us we would have to think for ourselves on the court. "There isn't going to be a play for every situation," he said. "You have to learn to recognize and react in the flow of the game. Observe. Anticipate. React. Finish!"

In one typical motion, Raj crossed midcourt and made two moves. First he passed to Roy on his right. Second, he moved to his left and set a screen for JJ. If the timing was right, JJ would have an open shot somewhere near the top of the paint. But the timing was never right.

"Rule number one for today," said Coach, "you have to move with a purpose. If you stand around after passing the ball, the offense stalls. Movement, movement, movement!" He clapped. "If nothing looks good, reset the offense and run it again until we get what we want."

There was a pause before Coach sent one of the white shirts to the bench. Then he grabbed me and said, "Go ahead, son. Get in there."

I nearly fell on my face running onto the court. After two days of standing on the sideline with Malcolm, this was my chance. I might have been a rookie, but I could play with anyone on that team, and now Roy Morelli and everyone else would see it. I only wished there had been time to slap hands with JJ before the whistle blew.

Coach waved me to the weak side, which meant the ball was going to come to me. *Movement, movement, movement. Catch and shoot or catch and pass.* My brain understood what to do, but my hands didn't. Instead of passing or shooting, I put the ball on the floor and dribbled.

Coach blew his whistle. "Wheeler, don't dribble— pass! Do it again!"

This time, I remembered to pass but forgot to move, and the offense got bunched up on one side of the court.

Again, Coach blew his whistle. "Wheeler!" he barked. "Don't just stand there—move to space! Do it again!"

On the third try, I remembered to pass. I remembered

to move. What I forgot was *where* to move. I was supposed to go left—toward the ball. I went right—away from the ball.

Coach marched over to me, took me by the elbow, and led me to the correct spot. Of course, this made everyone laugh, which just made Coach more upset, and he ordered us to the line for wind sprints. The whole team looked at me, disgusted. Some of them groaned. Roy glanced down the line at me and muttered, "You're killing me, Wheeler." Even JJ was avoiding eye contact. Not a high five or a nod. It was as though instead of giving him a reason to see me as an equal, I was giving him *new* reasons to see me as a chump. First, he was friends with the only eighth grader in Pilchuck who still wanted to trick-or-treat. Now he was friends with the rookie who couldn't find the right spot on the court with two hands and a flashlight. I was going backward. I had to play better.

On the fifth try, I finally got it right. Catch, pass, move with a purpose. Bing. Bang. Boom. When my screen led to an open jumper, Coach blew his whistle and clapped. "Good, Toby. You're getting it. We just might make a basketball player out of you yet." I was winded, but smiling. Ruben and Raj congratulated me, even though they were on the other team. Roy gave it up for me too—in his own way. "It's about time," he said as we caught our breath.

Next, Coach told us to start a full-court scrimmage. Now JJ and I were playing against each other, best friends matched up on opposing teams. Would I have an advantage others didn't because I knew his game, or would I be his latest victim? I wasn't sure. But being out there with him for some real up-and-down action, like we were back at the rec center, fired me up so much I almost forgot one of us was a benchwarmer. That feeling lasted about as long as it took Coach to say "Go!" What happened when the ball came to me was like a rec center game on fast forward. I had only held the ball for a second—barely time to open my eyes—when Raj and JJ closed in, shouting "Trap! Trap! Trap!" I panicked. Picked up the ball, then tossed it in the air like a hot potato and hoped whoever caught it was wearing a white jersey. A total rookie move, but what could I do? JJ had pounced on me. There was a look in his eyes I had never seen. Was it some competitive edge JJ saved for big moments, or had something about seeing me on the court in Pilchuck gym brought it out?

He didn't let up. And I tried not to back down. When Raj called motion, JJ was on the right wing, with me sticking him. I gave JJ space, knowing he would come off a screen and pass to Ruben—that was the play. But when JJ got the rock, he squared up and shot.

"Good, JJ," said Coach. "Toby, don't give him that kind of space."

Next possession. Same situation. Only this time, I played him tighter. JJ got the ball off the pass, shimmied left, shimmied right, then left again, around me, and straight to the hoop.

"Good, JJ," said Coach again. "Toby, not so tight."

It continued. JJ went through me, over me, by me, and under me. He never said a word. Just picked me apart with this Terminator look on his face.

"Hey, man," Ruben said to him when Coach wasn't listening. "Why don't you give the guy a break?"

"And someone else the ball," said Roy.

All JJ said was "I told you it wouldn't be like the rec center, Toby."

"I never said it would be."

"Yeah, but you thought it. I know you."

Maybe he was trying to prove a point. Team ball *was* a different game than pickup ball. And I was going to have to get used to running with guys who were faster, stronger, and better. Still, did he have to show me up in front of the whole team—and Coach?

Eventually, Coach called off the slaughter and we gathered in a circle at midcourt like we did at the end of every practice—after shooting free throws, of course. Raj had made two in a row so we got a one-day break from wind sprints. Everybody was pretty psyched about that—especially Khalil. Coach was about to send us to the locker room when the gym door opened and Megan entered. The sound of the door falling closed behind her made us all turn our heads.

Raj straightened his uniform.

Khalil sucked in his chest.

Roy stopped picking his teeth.

There was whispering and pointing, too.

Coach smiled and waved at Megan. "Hi, Champ," he called. "Be with you in a minute." *Champ?* I could tell some of the guys were ready to bust out laughing when they heard that one.

Megan looked at Coach, horrified. Her eyes grew to twice their normal size and her chin jutted forward in disbelief. Coach smiled back, sheepishly. Megan shook her head, then ducked into the gym office—but not before spying me and wiggling her fingers in my direction. Everybody who had been watching Megan spun their heads to face me.

"Looks like the benchwarmer's got a girlfriend," someone said.

Coach glared at me, his knuckles white on the clipboard.

What was Megan thinking? It's bad enough it took me five tries to run a simple play—now Coach thinks I'm putting the moves on his daughter! I had to say something. But what? "I'm her math tutor," I sputtered at last. "I'm helping her with algebra." I managed my best innocent face and looked up at Coach, who appeared to be doing some math of his own in his head. Something told me the equation he was solving went like this.

Toby with Megan in the hall + Megan waving at Toby in the gym = dead man on the end of the bench.

· 9 ·

The next day, Friday, Megan and I met in the cafeteria to work on math. We cleared some space at the end of a table along the back wall. The year before, JJ and I had sat at that same table, shoveling lunch down as quickly as possible so we could get outside and claim the one hoop with a net on the cracked basketball courts by the parking lot. When school started this year, two things had changed. First, the good hoop was gone, knocked down to make room for another portable classroom. Second, Valerie and Stephen began eating with us, which made me think that even if the hoop had still been there, we wouldn't have been racing outside to claim it. I was getting a little tired of watching Stephen and JJ pass songbooks back and forth like they were pricing baseball cards while Valerie went through her *mirror, mirror* routine. Helping Megan gave me an excuse to sit somewhere else, so it was a win-win situation, as long as Coach didn't show up and get the wrong idea.

Megan laid her book and papers on the table. The first sheet she showed me was a homework assignment. On the top of the page was her score: 3 for 10.

"The positives were no problem," she explained. "But the negatives gave me a hard time."

We went over her homework together.

Problem one was adding positives: 8 + 12 = 20. Megan got that right, obviously. Problem two was subtracting positives: 54 - 18 = 36. Right again. Easy. Problem number three was more addition: 5 + (-9) = -4.

"I understand that," said Megan. She pointed to her number line. "I just started at five and counted nine places to the left. But this is what I don't understand: negative five *minus* negative eight."

Her answer was negative thirteen.

"It's three," I said.

Megan scrunched her nose. The freckles bunched together. "How can a negative minus a negative be positive? I mean, if you have something negative and make it more negative, it should be *really* negative, right?"

"Not if you're taking it away," I said. "Think about it like this. If you take away something bad, it's actually good. Like on a team. If someone is being a pain and hurting the team, he's a negative. Right?"

Megan nodded. "Okay."

"So take him away from the team," I said. "Subtract the negative. And what do you have?"

"A better team, hopefully."

"Yeah—a positive."

After a while, Megan was feeling much better about positives and negatives. And I was starting to feel better about being in public with her. We talked for the rest of lunch, mostly about school and basketball. Hanging out with Megan was easy. It wasn't that I didn't see her as a girl—believe me, I did—it was just that unlike most girls, Megan never made me self-conscious, like there was something wrong with me. I could be myself around her, and that was pretty cool.

"How's the girls' team?" I asked.

Megan brightened. "I think we're gonna be pretty good," she said. "I hope people will come to our games." She chewed on a granola bar and surveyed the cafeteria. I did the same. A few tables over, the girls' team sat together, all of them wearing Pilchuck colors—green and white. Nearby, JJ sat with Valerie and Stephen at a four-person table, the fourth seat empty. Across the room, most of the basketball team was gathered around Ruben. Khalil and Roy were on his immediate right and left. Occasional bits of food flew back and forth with good-natured laughter.

At the other end of our table, Raj and McKlusky were really going at it about something. Raj was sitting ramrod-straight and slapping his palm on the surface with every third word. McKlusky was hunched over the table, wagging his finger. At first, I figured the argument was about this ongoing game of Risk they had been playing since June (and talking about every day before basketball practice), but the way the words *girls, date,* and *blast* kept popping up, it was clear we were way beyond world domination.

Finally, Raj turned away from McKlusky in disgust and said, as though she was his last hope, "*Megan,* you're a girl, right?"

"If not, I've been changing in the wrong locker room."

"Right," said Raj. "Well, maybe you can settle something. It's about the Winter Blast." Raj meant the dance at the end of January. I had skipped the Winter Blast the year before because there was a basketball game on TV that night. Also, I couldn't dance and I was sure I would embarrass myself trying.

Raj went on, "McKlusky says the reason nobody brings a date to the Winter Blast is that none of the girls want any of us to ask them. But *I* say the girls do want us to ask them, but we don't because chivalry is dead."

"Tell them what chivalry means," said McKlusky.

Raj looked at McKlusky impatiently. "They know what it means. Don't interrupt me."

"It means being a gentleman," said McKlusky.

"I know what it means," Megan assured him as he and Raj slid over. "And if you're asking me if I would want someone to ask me to the dance rather than just going by myself, the answer is it depends on who asked me."

"But you're not opposed to it in principle," Raj clarified.

"That's right," Megan agreed.

Raj slapped the table. "See," he said to McKlusky. "Girls *do* want to be asked. My cousin was right."

McKlusky shrugged. "Then why don't you ask her?"

"When the time is right," Raj answered as though he had explained this to McKlusky before.

"Ask who?" Megan asked, leaning in.

Raj folded his napkin. "Nobody," he said.

"Cassandra Miller," said McKlusky, pointing to a short girl with blond hair who was munching on an apple a few tables over.

"And I'm going with Melanie," he added, moving his finger one spot to the right, where a much taller girl with long dark hair was sitting.

"Cassandra and Melanie—from the basketball team?" Megan asked as Raj fumed at McKlusky for spilling his secret. "How do you know them?"

"We have science together," Raj explained.

"Cassandra told Raj he had a brilliant scientific mind," said McKlusky. "He's been in love ever since."

"I'm not in love," said Raj. "I just want to ask her to the dance."

"So why don't you?"

"I told you. I'm waiting for the right time!"

Megan gathered what remained of her lunch onto her tray and stood up. "Good for you, Raj," she said. "No sense rushing into anything. I mean, you do have *two months*."

"See," said Raj.

"So, Toby," McKlusky said after a minute. "Are you going to ask Megan?"

"Ask Megan what?"

"To the Winter Blast."

"No, he isn't going to ask Megan to the Blast. Are you out of your skull? She's Coach's *daughter*."

McKlusky polished off his drink. "So?"

"My cousin says you should never, ever get mixed up with the daughter of an authority figure. It's suicide."

"Your cousin?" I asked. "What is he—some kind of love expert?"

"He has three girlfriends. One of them is going to college."

Impressive. "Now?"

"In three years," Raj explained.

Not as impressive. Still, I pictured Raj's cousin. He had to be some older good-looking guy, maybe with a car and a closet full of cool clothes. And muscles, of course. "He really said that about authority figures?" I asked, remembering the way Coach had glared at me at the end of practice the day before.

Raj nodded. "Trust me, Toby. You're playing with fire if you let Megan get any ideas."

"Ideas about what?"

"About the two of you becoming . . . you know . . ."

"Whoa, whoa, whoa," I said, throwing my hands up. "Megan and I are just friends. She helped me win a basketball game; I help her with math. *That's it.* Besides," I went on, "even if I wanted to ask her to the dance, who's to say she would say yes? I mean, look at Melissa Calibrini. The only reason she said yes when I asked her if she wanted to see *Spider-Man* last year was because she *did* want to see it—just not with me."

"Whatever you say, Toby," Raj replied. "Just be careful."

• 10 •

Our first game was that night. After dinner, Dad drove me and Mom to the school gym. As we cruised down Verlot Street, Mom was on the phone with someone over at Landover Lumber.

"I don't care what Mr. Goodman thinks," she was saying. "You tell Mr. Goodman if Landover Lumber comes within a mile of those trees, I'll make sure his face is on the cover of every newspaper and magazine from here to Los Angeles. I'll fly in half of Hollywood and a school bus of smiling children and put them all in front of a TV camera if I have to. People in this town want a healthy river. And they do not want to look out their windows and see a barren hillside. Got it?"

I had heard these conversations a million times, but I was never sure whose side to take. The way Mom was attacking Landover Lumber, I could definitely see where my competitiveness came from, and I had to admire her for doing everything she could to win. But then there was Dad, stuck in the mud selling wood chips, which, to me, made him Warren Goodman's benchwarmer.

"Maureen," he said when Mom was off the phone, "do you really think you should be bluffing like that? I do work with these people."

"I thought we said we weren't going to let that get in the way."

"Well, it's complicated now. Warren is really going out of his way to get me that promotion. I know you have your job to do. But so do I. And it might help move things along if you weren't quite so adversarial."

"Phil, being nice isn't going to save the south slope."

"Neither is lying."

"I didn't lie."

"Who do you know in Hollywood?" Dad asked.

Mom was speechless, for once. Then she laughed. "I *could* know someone in Hollywood. Warren Goodman would never know the difference."

"He is dense," Dad agreed.

We were a few blocks from the school when they seemed to remember I was in the backseat. It was Mom who turned around to face me. "So, tonight's the big night," she said. "I finally get to see you in uniform."

"Mom, I probably won't even play. I'm the twelfth man, remember."

"The important thing is you're trying," she said.

I wondered what she would say if someone congratulated her for *trying* to save the south slope.

"I bet it's great being on the team with JJ, huh?" Dad asked. "You two used to spend so much time together."

"Sure, Dad," I said. The truth was that being on the team had not changed anything with JJ. He cruised through practice without saying much to anyone. At lunch, he sat with Stephen and Valerie. In his free time, he practiced guitar. So it was like it had been before basketball season, only now, instead of playing my game at the rec center, I was working like a dog in practice to . . . what . . . sit on the bench during games? Still, there were some good things about being on the team. Like walking into the gym after waving goodbye to Mom and Dad, and seeing the stands filling up with people who had come to watch us play basketball. . . . What's not to like about that?

Inside the locker room, I found JJ dressing by himself, his hair falling into his eyes when he leaned over to lace his shoes. I had just been at the barbershop that day. My hair was buzzed short. To me, if it was long enough to comb, it was too long.

"Game on," I said to JJ.

"Game on," said JJ. He held out his hand. "Listen, sorry about the other day in practice. I don't know what got into me. But, hey, I wouldn't have played that way if I didn't think you could handle it."

"I can handle it," I said, dropping my gym bag on

the floor. "Remember who has the record on the Hoop Shoot?"

"Are you going to hold that over me forever?" JJ asked, lacing his shoes. They were just like mine: mostly white with two blue streaks.

"Only until you beat me," I said, getting an idea. "Hey, we could go to Corner Pizza after the game tonight—what do you think?"

JJ had stood up and was putting his clothes in a locker. He took a deep breath.

The way he paused, I knew what he was going to say before he said it. "We don't have to if you don't want to," I went on, still hoping he *might* say yes.

JJ snapped the lock on his locker.

"I can't. But let's do something tomorrow. I'll meet you at the hoop. Around noon. We'll play some one-on-one."

"Yeah?"

JJ nodded. "Yeah."

Hoops. Tomorrow. Just me and JJ. The way it was supposed to be. I smiled and laced my shoes, knowing now that joining the team had been the right thing to do. I got even more excited when Raj came into the locker room and reported a full house. So long, gym rat; hello, star.

When we were all dressed, it was time for the pregame speech. Coach stood with JJ on his left and Ruben on his right. Ruben was bouncing on the balls of his feet, as though he might blast off from pent-up energy if the game didn't start soon. JJ was looking at his shoes. He flinched whenever Coach mentioned his name.

"Keep it simple out there," Coach said. "Talk on defense. Make smart passes. And remember to run your offense through JJ like we've done all week." He looked at JJ. "Menzel Lake may open in a zone. If they do, wait for the double-team and look for the open man." Coach tapped the board with his stick of chalk. "Anyone have anything to add?"

Ruben stepped forward. Well, bounced forward. He held out his hand. We put ours on top of his. "Everyone else in this league thinks we belong in the basement," he began. "Well, we don't. Not anymore. The only things that belong in the basement are rats and stuff nobody wants and I don't see any rats or junk here. We're gonna shock the world this season. Let's get it started tonight."

"Chuckers!" we all cheered before leaving the locker room.

The jersey felt cool on my skin as we waited in the tunnel. Over the jerseys we wore warm-up shirts. Most of the guys had nicknames printed on the back of their shirts. Only two shirts were blank: mine and Malcolm's. The shorts hung to an inch above my knees—just right. We were ready to go. The house lights dimmed. A single spotlight danced on the court. The capacity crowd filling the Pilchuck gym cheered and stomped. In a moment, the starters would be announced. Then the rest of us would follow.

Khalil strolled out first. Then Roy. Ruben bounced after them. Raj was next, with JJ on his heels bringing a roar from above as the announcer sang, "JJ Fosssssterrrrr!" I wished I could have run out there with him. There were only ten guys between us in the lineup, but it felt like a hundred. Then it was time for the second team. Each player ran from the tunnel and passed through a gauntlet of teammates with high fives all around. I moved toward the edge of the tunnel, but Coach held me back. "Not yet," he said as McKlusky took the court. "Not yet," he said again as the introductions continued. By now, the roar was fading. "Not yet," he said as Malcolm hopped out of the tunnel. Then it was just me and Coach.

Coach smiled and pushed me on. "Go ahead, Toby. This is your moment."

He was right. It was my moment. That was *my* name the announcer had called. So what if I was the last one into the gym? So what if I didn't have a nickname? It was my first day as a superstar. I took a deep breath and got ready to soak up the applause.

There was just one problem. By the time my name was called, the gauntlet was ancient history. The other players were warming up, shooting jumpers and free throws. The crowd was no longer watching the court, either. People in the stands were too busy saving seats, waving to friends, or standing in line at the snack stand to care about a benchwarmer making his grand entrance. Disappointed, I grabbed a ball from the rack and joined my teammates at the other end of the gym. The buzz I had felt walking into the gym had worn off in an instant.

Soon the horn blew. Coach gathered us for one last pep talk, then sent the starters to the floor for the tip-off. I made the long walk to the end of the bench to sit between Malcolm and Megan. Coach was letting her sit on the bench during games to take notes.

Megan smiled when she saw me. "Hey, it's the twelfth man!" she said as the players were shaking hands on the court. She was wearing jeans and a green T-shirt and holding a notepad. There was a pencil behind her ear.

"Please don't call me that," I said.

"Wow," said Megan. "Who'd have guessed a bench-warmer could be so sensitive?" At our feet, the game was under way.

JJ began the game on fire. A reverse layup along the baseline. A crossover dribble drive. A runner in traffic. And of course, the stop-and-pop. It was a clinic, and Menzel Lake was getting schooled. I could hear the fans behind me take a deep breath whenever JJ had the ball, as if they knew that in a moment he would give them a reason to let it out in a cheer. Ruben and the others had little to do, and they began to look bored. JJ *was* doing most of the work on offense, but not because he was selfish. He was just following orders. Coach had told us a hundred times the offense should go through JJ on every possession. The only problem was, nobody was setting the screens JJ needed for open shots. It was like

Ruben, Roy, and Khalil had made up their minds if they weren't going to get to shoot, they didn't want to do the other stuff.

At least *they* were in the game. As we came back to the court for the second half—the other guys sweaty from running up and down the court, and me clean and dry—I was starting to feel like a fan who had won really good seats in a radio contest. Once or twice I looked down and was surprised to see I was wearing a uniform. I had to keep reminding myself I was on the team too. I had joined the team to show everyone that a gym rat could play *real* basketball. But here I was again sitting down watching JJ play without me. Nothing had changed.

"It shouldn't be this close," said Megan a few minutes into the fourth quarter. She was shaking her head. We had been unable to shake Menzel Lake. Their zone was smothering JJ, and without any help from Ruben and the others, there was no outlet when he found himself double- or triple-teamed. Worse, on offense, their best player—Gallagher—was heating up.

"Gallagher is too good," I said. "He has sixteen points and there are still five minutes left."

Megan agreed. "And he has his teammates involved. Every one of their starters has scored. It's no surprise they're playing hard on defense, too."

"They're triple-teaming JJ," I said to Megan. "Is that even legal?"

"That's their zone," she explained. "The problem is they're also closing the passing lanes so JJ can't find the open man."

Sure enough, Raj passed to JJ on the wing. The second JJ had the ball, the Knights swarmed. JJ did his best to wiggle through the defense, but with so many hands reaching for the ball, not even a ghost could have escaped. The trap forced a turnover and the Knights had the ball back, down by two, with two minutes to play.

"Come on, guys, this is our game!" Raj urged during a time-out. All the players were circled around Coach, who was holding his clipboard and loosening his tie.

"You should get up too," Megan whispered to me.

I stood and joined the huddle.

"You've got to think out there!" Coach said. "Stay with the offense!" Behind him, the cheerleaders were doing their best to reignite the crowd, but the Menzel Lake comeback had everyone uneasy. "JJ will take you home!"

"Coach?"

"Yes, Ruben."

"I just wanted to say . . . they're leaving Roy open on the low post to double JJ. If we look inside, we might get some easy baskets."

Coach patted Ruben on the shoulder. "The only way we can get the ball inside is if the rest of you start setting screens. I see too much standing around out there. You should be in constant motion. Move with a purpose!

Help each other out on defense. They've been running that pick-and-roll all night. You're not going to stop it unless you communicate."

We put our hands together. "Chuckers!"

"You can do it," I said to JJ, whose only response was a distracted nod. His eyes were on his father, who was standing with his arms crossed near the exit. JJ seemed spellbound. Only at the sound of the whistle did he finally manage to tear his eyes free. I wondered if JJ was remembering all the games the year before, when his dad would chew out some official whose only mistake had been to call a foul on JJ. Or was he thinking ahead to what might happen if we let this game get away?

Thirty seconds later, the comeback was complete. Menzel Lake set a screen for Gallagher, who caught the ball, curled, and buried a three. JJ, who had been guarding Gallagher all night, never saw the screen, and nobody called it out.

We failed to score on our next possession but stopped the Knights on theirs. Coach had used his last time-out, so there was no way to set up a play. The decisions would have to be made on the court. We had twenty seconds to score. We were down by one.

Raj crossed midcourt as the clock ticked down to ten. JJ ran along the baseline trying to shake his defender. With seven seconds left, Raj swung the ball to Roy just as JJ popped open in the corner. But rather than pass, Roy launched an off-target three as time ran out. The shot missed and we lost. Feeling useless, I followed the rest of the team to the locker room, where we sat silently, listening to Coach.

"We aren't going to be successful without team-work," he said. "I didn't see any movement tonight. No screens. No spacing. I saw four of you standing around watching JJ. We need to do better. It takes twelve of you to win one game."

News to me, Coach.

· 11 ·

I woke up excited. The game had not gone our way, but it was a new day. After breakfast, I looked out the window. The sun was breaking through a thin layer of clouds. It was a few minutes before twelve. There was no sign of JJ yet. I went out and began shooting, hoping the sound of the basketball would draw him out of his house. Instead, it was the sound of music coming from his basement that drew me in.

I climbed the steps to JJ's house and crossed the porch. A row of planters sat on the ground. I remembered when JJ's mom had herbs and vegetables growing in them. Now that she was in California, the planters were empty, except for a few grains of soil. I stood at the door, unsure of what to do. I knocked a few times, but no one answered.

The door was unlocked, so I took a deep breath and went inside and down the steps to the basement. It was empty. Just a few beanbags, an old couch, a Ping-Pong table, and some stereo equipment JJ had bought at a garage sale. Leaning against a large speaker was a guitar. A set of drums sat nearby. On the couch were a pink sweater and an old green hat. Why were Stephen and Valerie in the house when JJ was supposed to be outside with me? I was tiptoeing back up the stairs when I heard voices in the kitchen. Suddenly the door at the top of the stairs opened. The lights came on and I saw Stephen, with JJ and Valerie behind him.

"Toby!" said Stephen, his hair spilling into his eyes. "When did you get here?"

Valerie stepped around me cautiously. JJ seemed surprised to see me. "Toby," he said. "What are you *doing* here?"

Standing there in the basement wearing shorts and holding a basketball, I felt out of place among JJ and his new friends. What *was* I doing there?

"It's noon," I said. I started to act out a game of one-on-one before remembering how well my trick-or-treating performance had gone over on Halloween. Instead I got right to the point. "I thought we were playing ball."

"We're sort of in the middle of practicing," JJ explained.

In the middle of practicing? Personal foul for blowing off hoops!

"You want to hear us play?" Stephen asked. "We could use an audience."

Valerie plopped herself on the couch. "What about me?"

"You're just a groupie," Stephen replied. "You *have* to like us."

"Don't call me a groupie or I'll tell Mark you've been skipping class to hang out behind the school."

Stephen flicked a guitar pick at Valerie. "Stop calling him Mark."

"Sorry," Valerie answered. "I mean *your dad*."

"Anyway," Stephen added, "does *Sheila* know you flunked gym class?"

Valerie crossed her arms dramatically and fell back against the couch. "It's not my fault. Badminton is hard."

Just then, JJ strummed his guitar and a deep groan came from the banged-up amp in the corner. Stephen and Valerie fell quiet as JJ played a few more chords. He was focused on his fingers and the strings. I had played enough basketball with him to know that look—he was blocking out everything else. Only now, instead of focusing on dribbling and shooting, his mind was on guitar. Without a word, Stephen began rapping his sticks against the faces of the drums. As the slow, deep chords picked up pace and became high-pitched, the drumbeat accelerated too, until the rhythm sounded like a guard trying to shake his man with a crossover. That was as good as it got. Before long, Stephen was pounding his sticks to one beat while JJ's fingers slid up and down the guitar until they sounded like someone playing the recorder for the first time. There were no words, either, just three minutes of ear-splitting jamming.

"What do you think?" JJ asked when he was done.

"What do I think?" I was stalling. The truth was they were terrible. If JJ had played basketball like he played guitar, we never would have won a game all year. But the smile in his voice told me JJ had no idea how bad he was, and I was not about to be the one to tell him they sounded like a bag of cats. If I did, we'd never get outside.

"Awesome," I said.

"Awesome is right," said Stephen.

High five.

Valerie sat on the couch. "I think you guys sound like a car accident."

"I thought groupies were supposed to like everything a band did," said JJ, laying down the guitar.

Valerie grabbed his hands and twisted them. "Who are you calling a groupie?" she said, laughing.

"So, who else is in the band?" I asked.

"Just us," said Stephen. "JJ on guitar and yours truly on drums." He twirled a drumstick in his fingers.

"Who sings?"

"We both do," JJ answered.

Yikes.

Suddenly Stephen thrust the drumsticks at me. "You wanna try?" he asked, gesturing to the seat.

"We should probably practice," said JJ. "My dad will be home in an hour."

On the couch, Valerie sat up. "JJ, you shouldn't be so afraid of him. Just tell him you like playing guitar and let him deal with it. What's he gonna do, send you to military school?"

JJ picked up a sheet of music. "I wouldn't be surprised."

By then, Stephen had led me to the seat. "Don't sweat it. It'll just take a minute. Besides, what if I get injured?" he said, putting his arm around me. "We might need a backup."

JJ shrugged. Next to him, Valerie glanced down at her empty cup. "You guys can practice all you want," she said. "I'm getting another Coke."

"Hold on," JJ said. "I'll go with you."

Holding the sticks, I started banging on the drums. Stephen stopped me.

"Slide your hands back," he said. "And hold the stick loosely between your thumb and two front fingers."

The sticks rapped against the drums, starting with a simple beat. After a minute of drumming, I finished with one last *whack,* then flipped the sticks into the air, meaning to catch them like batons. One stick went straight up in the air, then fell harmlessly to my lap. But the other stick flew sideways toward the stairs. If my finale had been a half second earlier, the stick would have hit the steps below Valerie's feet and rolled to the ground. Instead, it caught the lip of her cup full force, spilling Coke on her pants and shoes.

"Good thing it wasn't hot chocolate," I said.

"Toby," JJ said, embarrassed.

"Maybe I should go," I said, picking up my basketball. They all looked at me like I was from another planet. Stephen retrieved his drumsticks and coughed. Valerie bared her teeth. This was not good.

JJ walked me to the door. I switched the ball from my right hand to my left, then back to my right. "Okay, um, well, just let me know when you want to play. Maybe when you're done practicing, we can meet out front."

"We're gonna be here for a while."

"But you said your dad was coming home."

"And then we're going out for a while."

"Where?"

"Just out," JJ said impatiently. "Man, Toby. You sound like my dad."

"Sorry. I thought we were gonna play ball."

"We play ball every day."

"Maybe *you* do," I said.

"Nobody forced you to join the team, so don't start complaining now just because you're not playing."

I felt the basketball in my hands. I just wanted to get out of there. "You know you shouldn't make plans with someone if you're not going to keep them."

"Great," JJ said. "First Valerie. Now you, too. Why is everyone telling me what to do?"

I started to say that maybe Valerie was right. I knew *I* was. But JJ was getting annoyed and once someone was annoyed, that person wasn't going to be convinced of *anything*.

Later, I shot by myself, building steam with every jumper. I kept thinking about JJ inside with Valerie and

Stephen. It was the second time in two weeks I had been left on the street. Ditched for a band. Stood up. Abandoned. And what had I done about it? Nothing. That was what. Just stood there and taken it like a chump. But why? I didn't put up with any garbage from Vinny Pesto. Why should I take it from JJ? And that was when it hit me. I didn't have to. As my last shot rattled in, I decided that starting Monday I wasn't going to spend any more time wondering where JJ was or what he was doing. If JJ wanted to be friends, that was fine, but he would have to come to me.

When the sun had gone behind the clouds and the rain began to fall again, I took my ball and went inside the house. Mom and Dad were having an unscheduled family meeting in the kitchen. They were standing on opposite sides of the island, Dad in jeans and a T-shirt, Mom in the clothes she wore to the gym.

"Do you know what's going to happen at Landover Lumber if the company can't harvest those trees? A lot of people could lose their jobs, Maureen."

Mom was ready with an answer. "Phil, clearing those trees is going to devastate the salmon run across the entire watershed. Is that really worth saving a few jobs that aren't going to be around much longer anyway?"

"Cutting the south slope might not affect those rivers at all."

"Might not affect them at all?" Mom repeated. "Are you kidding me? Did you hear that from Warren?"

"Maureen."

Mom stared at Dad. Dad stared back.

"Are you going to lose your job, Dad?" I asked. He shook his head.

"Will you still get the promotion?"

He shook his head again. "I don't know." Sighing, he left the kitchen.

I stayed downstairs and fixed myself a sandwich. I thought about Dad. He seemed worried, but I knew he would find a way to get that promotion. The question was, could I find a way to get myself off the bench?

• 12 •

On Monday afternoon, Pilchuck was wrapped in thick layers of fog that rolled off the mountains and drenched everything it touched. If the weather was going to be this cold, I thought as I ran across the courtyard from the school to the gym, I wished it would just snow. That reminded me of Megan. The first day we met she had asked if it snowed in Pilchuck. For her sake, I hoped it would. Picturing her smiling made me do the same, which must have made me look like a lunatic as I walked into practice dripping wet, sneezing, and smiling stupidly.

For once, I didn't stand alone waiting for JJ to join me at the beginning of practice. Instead, while he warmed up alone in the corner, I stretched with Raj and McKlusky. They were talking about a banner that had appeared that morning across the front of the stage in the cafeteria. It was white with frosty blue writing and a picture of a cold wind blowing through a mountain pass. It said: WINTER BLAST—DANCE AND TALENT SHOW: JANUARY 21ST! The appearance of the banner had created some buzz around the school, even though the dance was in January and this was still mid-November. In a couple of days, I bet, the talk would die down and everyone would move on to something else. Well, almost everyone.

Raj psyched himself up as he reached for his toes. "Tomorrow," he said. "Tomorrow I will ask Cassandra Miller to the dance."

"Sure you will," said McKlusky.

"Are you calling me a chicken?"

"It's just like Risk," McKlusky said. He did an imitation of Raj, which meant speaking very crisply—like a Spanish teacher introducing a new word. "Tomorrow I'm going to conquer South America. Tomorrow I'm going to move more armies to Madagascar. Tomorrow I'm going to ask Cassandra to the dance. But you never do. You never do."

I laughed as Raj and McKlusky went on and on about Risk. Behind them, I saw JJ knocking down jumpers on the court. Catch. Square up. Elevate. Release. Swish. Catch. Square up. Elevate. Release. Swish. He was automatic, all right, but what good was it if he wasn't having any fun? At least Raj and McKlusky seemed to enjoy themselves, even when they were arguing.

"Have you asked Melanie yet?" Raj asked, grabbing a ball from the rack.

"I will as soon as you ask Cassandra."

Raj sniffed. "Why do I have to go first?"

"Because Melanie might not want to go with me unless she knows Cassandra is going with you."

"Did it ever occur to you Cassandra might feel the same way?" Raj asked.

That was when some of the other guys joined the conversation.

"If you two are talking about the dance," said Roy, "you better move quick. Girls don't like to be kept waiting."

"Don't listen to him," Khalil added. "You gotta take your time. Make sure you ask right. Otherwise you're gonna get . . . *rejected*!" Khalil brought his arm up, then waved it forward like he was swatting away a layup.

"Man, you can't even run a lap without wheezing," Ruben joked. "How are you gonna dance for an hour?"

"Like this," said Khalil.

We all watched and laughed as Khalil danced around the gym. It was the first time I felt like I was a part of the team. Nobody was mad at me for screwing up. I wasn't standing in the corner. Was this what Dad thought he was missing by not playing sports?

When Khalil was done dancing, Roy said, "So, when are you gonna pop the question to Coach's daughter?"

A second passed before I realized he was talking to me. "When am *I* going to ask Coach's daughter? *Me?*"

"You're always with her," Ruben said. "Eating lunch.

Sitting on the end of the bench. You think we don't notice this stuff? It's obvious, man."

"What's obvious?"

"That she *likes* you," said Roy.

"I told you," said Raj.

"That's not what you told me. You told me getting mixed up with the daughter of an authority figure was suicide."

"Actually, my cousin said that."

"Whatever!" I turned back to the team. "The point is, you can all relax because even if Megan does like me, which she doesn't, there is no way I'm taking her to the Blast or anywhere else there might be dancing."

There was no response, so I went on, "I had a bad experience. In fifth grade. We had to learn ballroom dancing and since there were too many boys I had to dance with Lester the Bulge. He broke two of my toes with his boots and dropped me on the dip. The PE teacher said I was the first person he ever had to send to the nurse with a dancing injury."

They all stared at me.

Finally Roy waved his hand. "Oh, please, you know you wanna ask her."

"You like her." Khalil nodded.

"No doubt about it, baby," Malcolm said. "Megan's your girlfriend."

Suddenly, from behind us, we heard *shrieeeek* as Coach forced every molecule of oxygen from his lungs into his whistle. "Wheeler," he barked as he handed me a basketball. "On the line."

Red in the face, I skulked to the free-throw line. As far as I could tell, the three smacks of the ball against the gym floor before I shot were the sound of a dead man dribbling.

· 13 ·

Our second game was that Friday against Cedar Crest. I had played better in practice that week, but it still seemed like I was always in the wrong place at the wrong time on the court or doing some little thing incorrectly—like using a chest pass when I should have used a bounce pass. And Coach never missed a chance to let me hear about it. For a benchwarmer, I sure was getting an awful lot of heat. I wished Malcolm had kept his mouth shut on Monday about Megan being my girlfriend. I was getting restless on the bench. I wanted to get in an actual game, but if Coach thought there *was* some funny business between me and his daughter, then Raj and his cousin were right: I had no hope of ever leaving the bench. Even worse, our game against Hamilton was a week away. One look at me on the bench and Vinny Pesto would humiliate me.

The Cedar Crest game was close from the start. Both teams played physical basketball, and the refs were swallowing their whistles. The Cougars kept a hand in JJ's face everywhere he went. He never saw a ray of daylight. He did his best to get off his shots, but with the slapping, the pulling, and the hand checks, most of them were off target. It didn't help that Raj had four turnovers. "Where's your head, Raj?" Coach shouted more than once.

Luckily, Ruben was a monster in the paint, shaking off guys twice his size for second-chance points. Thanks to him, we were still in it with seven minutes left in the fourth quarter.

"Coach," said Roy during the next time-out, "they're all over us. Can't you say something to the refs?"

Shaking his head, Coach shouted, "Nothing you or I say to the refs is going to change the way the game is called! Just play your game. Take what the refs give you. If the other team pushes, push back. Contest *every* shot. Fight for every loose ball."

"Their big men are too big. They're like cedar trees," Khalil gasped. "They're shooting right over us."

Everybody began talking at once. Except me. Coach held up his hands for quiet.

That was when I said, "They look tired."

Everybody stared at me.

"Go on, Toby," said Coach.

"They look tired. They've got their hands on their knees."

"What are you saying?" Ruben asked.

What *was* I saying? My brain raced to catch up with my mouth. What do you do to a tired team in a close game? "We should press," I said. "We've been running all those wind sprints. We might as well use the stamina."

"He's right," said JJ. "We *should* press. Take them out of their half-court game. Force some turnovers."

"Good call," said Ruben. Everyone else nodded. For the first time, I felt like I was more important to the team than the ball rack.

Coach looked around the huddle. "Okay," he said to everybody's surprise, "let's try a full-court press for three minutes. One-three-one. Raj at one point. Ruben, McKlusky, and Roy in the middle. Then JJ. Khalil, you take a breather."

Khalil covered his head with a towel. "Phew."

Who knows? I thought as the team took the court again. Maybe they would build enough of a lead to get me in the game. Sure enough, the pace of the game accelerated. Both teams were trapping, stealing, and scoring off fast breaks.

We stayed ahead. With three minutes left, Cedar Crest inbounded the ball on the baseline to their center. He looked like a pair of stilts with arms and a head. As soon as Stilts caught the pass, Ruben and Raj raced over, yelling, "Trap, trap, trap!" Stilts panicked. Unable to dribble, he threw the ball up in the air like a hot brick. Ruben scooped it up and dashed to the hoop for two.

Ruben hopped sideways down the sideline, flapping

his arms and nodding his head. He wasn't showboating, exactly. He was playing to the crowd—to get them into the game.

We had the crowd. We had momentum.

The only things not going our way were the whistles.

"I think the ref must have a kid who goes to Cedar Crest," I said to Megan after JJ was called for a touch foul, his fourth.

"One more and JJ is out of the game," Megan said.

A minute later Raj was leading another fast break with JJ trailing. A step inside the free-throw line, he tossed the ball over his back into JJ's hands, then stepped aside. That was when the Cedar Crest center moved into JJ's path. There was a collision. The whistle blew. Then came the call: offensive foul.

Outrageous.

JJ was out of the game.

"Open your eyes, ref. You're missing a great game," I called.

Megan lowered her eyes. "Oh no, Toby."

Suddenly the ref ran up to our bench, blew his whistle, and said, "Technical foul on Pilchuck, number . . ." He looked at me. I was still wearing my warm-up shirt. "What's your number, son?" he asked.

"I . . ."

Malcolm lifted my shirt up. "Thirty-two," he said.

"Two shots!" said the ref.

I couldn't believe it. The first time my number had been called during a game and it was for this! Suddenly,

I went from the invisible man to the man everyone wanted to pound into pulp.

"Oh, man!" Roy cried. "You gotta be kidding me."

"That was not cool," Khalil added.

"Not cool," Ruben said.

Coach turned bright red so quickly, Megan had to run to him with a glass of water and tell him to sit until he caught his breath.

JJ wouldn't even look at me. He was on the court, staring at the scoreboard and shaking his head.

Cedar Crest made the first free throw to pull within six. The second free throw was short. Khalil, who subbed in when JJ fouled out, got a hand on the rebound before the Cougars came up with possession. The Cedar Crest center pump-faked. Khalil leaned in, bumping him. The shot went up and fell in.

The whistle blew.

And one.

The lead was down to four.

After the free throw, the lead was down to three.

What had I done?

We never recovered. Cedar Crest seized the momentum. Ruben fought until the last second, but we ended up losing by four. The buzzer blew and the Cougars danced into the visitors' locker room. The rest of my team stood near the court, dazed, before wandering away to change. I sat right where I had sat all night and would probably sit until the end of the season—on the end of the bench.

Behind me, the stands were emptying. Mom tapped me on the shoulder to tell me she and Dad would be waiting for me in the parking lot. Megan sat next to me tapping her feet on the wood floor. I guess there wasn't much to say to a guy who had blown the game without even taking off his warm-up shirt.

JJ had just taken the seat on the other side of me when a voice tore through the half-empty gym. Across the court, JJ's dad had cornered a man half his size: the ref who had whistled JJ for the fifth foul. "Don't tell *me* the rules," he growled. "I saw what was going on out there tonight."

The ref tried to wiggle free.

"Are you blind?"

Most of the people left in the gym had turned their attention to the altercation. Inches now separated the ref from JJ's dad. I had never seen a grown man punch another in real life.

Tossing aside his towel, JJ rose from his seat. He crossed the court and pulled his dad away, and to the relief of the ref, they left the gym.

"That was scary," said Megan, gripping my wrist. She was trembling. Speaking of scary, walking our way from the scorer's table was Coach Applewhite. Seeing that the situation with JJ's dad was under control, he was looking for Megan.

I only had a few seconds.

Using my left hand to pry Megan's hand from my wrist, I said, "You know, I really should be going."

It was too late. Coach locked his eyes on me and said, "Wheeler, for crying out loud, what did I say earlier?"

Megan slipped away. She was right. I was toast.

"Sorry, Coach," I said.

"Wheeler, if you can't learn to follow instructions, how can I ever put you in a game? I told you it takes twelve of you to win and I meant it. You may not like your role but you still have a job to do. So you decide: Play by my rules or find something else to do with your time."

· 14 ·

Six days after Coach warned me to play by the rules, I was standing in a gravel parking lot at the state park with the rest of the eighth-grade class. We had just gotten off the bus, and everyone was scrambling around, gathering in groups, including Megan and Valerie. They had become friendly the day they had covered for each other in the hallway, and during the ride from school to the park had made plans to collect pine boughs together. That was our assignment for the afternoon. We were all supposed to collect one armful of fallen branches with the needles still on them. Then we were going to go back to school and weave wreaths for the retirement home, the fire station, the library, and other places that already had Christmas decorations coming out the wazoo.

"Toby!" Megan called. "Do you want to come with

us?" She was wearing a red fleece jacket and yellow rain pants. If her shoes had been green instead of brown, she would have looked like a stoplight. As she waved, my mouth went a little dry. Yes, I wanted to go with them! But hovering nearby were JJ and Stephen. I reconsidered. Even with the invitation from Megan, I still would have felt like I was tagging along.

Twenty minutes later I was hiking with Raj through damp underbrush on the edge of a mountain trail. The air was chilly and there was nowhere to hide from the rain, but anything was better than being in class. And despite the cool, drippy weather, I was already sweating underneath my parka as I told Raj what had happened after the game the past Friday.

When I got to the part about Megan grabbing my wrist, Raj said, "Your wrist? That's bad."

"But what Coach saw was me lifting her hand off."

Raj shook his head. "What did I tell you, Toby? Coach sees what he wants to see."

I pushed back a shoulder-high branch and stepped around the tree. "Vinny was right," I said under my breath. "I'm never going to get off the bench."

"*Ow!*" Behind me, Raj was brushing pine needles and sap from his face. "Watch it," he said.

"Sorry," I said.

"That's okay." Raj bent down to pick up a bough. We had stumbled into a pretty good pile of them. "Who's Vinny?" he asked.

I told Raj about my vow to Vinny Pesto.

"Let me get this straight," he said. "We have to beat Hamilton in the championship game?"

"And I have to be on the court. I forgot to mention that."

"We're 0 and 2, Toby!" Raj said as if he needed to remind me. "If we lose two more games, we aren't even going to make the play-offs. What else did you promise him?"

"Only that I would hit the winning shot in his face."

"So all we have to do is win seven of the next games, get our twelfth man on the court in the championship, and have him hit a last-second shot?"

"In Vinny Pesto's face," I added.

Raj whistled. "Good luck," he said.

"What am I going to do?" I asked, hopping over a small stream running through a stand of sagging fir trees.

Raj took off his raincoat, laid it across a stump, and sat with a sigh. I did the same. We were just a few feet from the trail now.

"Take it one step at a time," Raj said. "The first thing you have to do is make sure Coach knows there is nothing happening between you and Megan." He gave me a look. "Which is the truth, right?"

"Um, as far as I know."

"Good," Raj said. "After that, all you have to do is make up for what happened against Cedar Crest."

"How do I do that?"

"I'm not sure," Raj admitted as he blew on his hands.

"But we better think of something fast. Our game against Hamilton is Friday."

I looked up, admiring the heights of the trees around me. Even though it wasn't exactly tropical in the foothills of the mountains, I did like living so close to the wilderness. It made me feel like I was always a few minutes away from an adventure. It was at moments like these that I saw things Mom's way and wanted to save every acre of forest possible. But I had also seen the old photographs on the walls in the library and come away believing that cutting down trees was just part of the history here. Like fishing in Alaska or making movies in Hollywood. I was just glad Mom and Dad never made me choose sides at home.

I was just picking up a pinecone to chuck at Raj when two people came down the trail—Melanie, ducking under overhanging branches, and Cassandra, high-stepping over roots and logs. Raj caught sight of Cassandra and turned sheet-white. I think if he had had time, he would have jumped behind the nearest tree. But Cassandra saw him and walked right over.

"Hi, Raj," she said. "How's it going?"

"Hi, Cassandra," he said too loudly. "What are you doing here?"

Melanie and I smiled at each other.

Cassandra looked down at the branches in her hand. "Same as you, I guess. Collecting pine boughs."

"Oh—right."

"Well," Cassandra said after about two minutes, "I guess I'll see you later at school."

"Or on the bus," Raj blurted.

Oh, man, this guy was worse than me. How was he ever going to ask this girl to a dance? She might have to do it for him.

Cassandra started to leave, then stopped like she had remembered something she wanted to say. "Hey," she said, "you guys should come to one of our games some-time. They're a lot of fun."

Raj bobbled his chin. "Yeah—okay," he said.

Melanie followed Cassandra. "Bye, Toby. Bye, Raj. Say hi to McKlusky."

When they were out of sight, Raj took a deep breath and said to me, "Well, I think that went pretty well."

There was no time to discuss his "conversation" with Cassandra because a moment later, Megan came around the corner with Valerie. Laughing, Megan tucked her branches under one arm and waved.

"Here comes trouble," said Raj.

"You're making a big deal out of nothing."

"We'll see."

Behind the girls came JJ, bearing two armloads of pine boughs. He made his way past the roots of a fallen tree, balancing carefully because he had no free hands. He nodded when he saw me, then kept going.

"How's it going?" Megan asked me. She had stopped to tie her shoe.

"Not bad. Your dad made me do extra sprints yesterday."

Megan smiled. "It just means he cares."

"If he really cared, he would let me play. Of course, he might have to tape my mouth shut first."

Megan stepped onto a rock to cross the small stream. "Why do you think he asked me to sit on the bench during your games?"

"I don't know," I said, pretending to think hard about the question, "maybe he thought you needed some help adding up the score."

"I can add up the points you've scored so far this season." Megan reached down from the rock to punch my shoulder. "Zero," she said, and started to slip. She waved her arms around for balance, and then toppled into me before landing on the wet ground.

"What do you know?" said Valerie. "Toby Wheeler actually prevented an injury. That's a first."

Megan was unhurt, but she was half-soaked. I handed her my parka. "Here. I was sweating anyway."

"Gross," said Valerie.

"Thanks, Toby," Megan said. Shivering, she replaced her wet jacket with the parka.

"No problem," I said, holding back a branch. "There's another pile of boughs just up here past this tree."

Megan walked by me. I let go of the branch and followed her.

From behind us came a thwack and then, *"Yeowww!"*

I turned around. Valerie was brushing pine needles from her face. A large red mark ran across her cheek.

Not again! Valerie was still glaring at me when Raj came over. "What are you doing?" he whispered frantically.

"It was an accident. I didn't know she was there."

"Not that," he said, pointing past Valerie. *"That."*

"Megan?"

"Yes! Why did you give her your coat?"

"Her jacket was wet. What's the big deal?"

Raj sounded very disappointed in me. "My cousin says when a girl borrows a piece of clothing from a guy it means she likes him. You were supposed to make her *not* like you. Then you come along with a dry raincoat and save her. What were you thinking?"

"She looked cold."

Raj trudged away through the fallen branches. "You've done it now, Toby. I tried to warn you. But you've done it now."

· 15 ·

The next day I was standing in the hallway during lunch. In a few hours we were traveling to Hamilton Middle School for a showdown with the Harriers—and Vinny Pesto. Beating them would be tough, but at least we still had a chance to save our season.

My personal outlook was not so good. I was one more misstep from blowing any chance of ever getting into a game. Which was why when Raj came to me with the note from Megan, I took it seriously.

Thanks again for the parka. That was very sweet. I had to leave school for a few hours to do something. See you after the game maybe.

—M

"Who gave you this?"

"It's from your girlfriend," said Raj. "She asked me to give it to you."

"How many times do I have to tell you? Megan is *not* my girlfriend."

"Look, Toby," said Raj. "It doesn't make any difference to me what you do. But if you want to stay on Coach's good side, you need to end this right now."

"You make it sound like it's an emergency," I said.

Raj put his hand on my shoulder. "Toby, I talked to my cousin. He says you've already passed the third stage."

"The third stage?"

"The first stage is hand-on-hand contact. You passed the second stage when you lent her clothing. Now you've moved on to notes with just initials—the third stage."

"I give up," I said. "What do I do?"

"Something like this happened to my cousin once. His girlfriends send him notes all the time."

"What did he do?"

Raj looked at his watch. "Do you have a pencil and paper? You have to let her down. But you have to let her down easy so she doesn't get mad and make things even worse."

Although my gut told me Raj was not exactly Pilchuck Middle School's number one expert on girls, I listened to his advice. I had no choice. I had to get on Coach's good side if I wanted to get in the game.

"Okay. What else?" I asked.

"Write her a note," said Raj. "Notes are better than meeting in person. No big scenes."

"What should I say?"

"Tell her you just want to be friends. But give her a reason. Girls *always* need a reason."

A moment later, I fished a pencil from my bag and wrote:

M
Can we just be friends? I think you-know-who
would want it that way.
*   —T*

"Good," said Raj. "But it might help if you wrote something nice about her too."

M
Can we just be friends? I think you-know-who
would want it that way. You have a nice smile.
*   —T*

"Too nice," said Raj.

I thought for a moment, then wrote:

M
Can we just be friends? I think you-know-who
would want it that way. You have a pretty nice
smile.
*   —T*

Raj read the note. "Perfect."

"Will you give it to her?" I asked. "I don't want her to read it in front of me."

"I'm not going to see her again today. But McKlusky has social studies with her fifth period. I'll give it to him and he can give it to her."

"Thanks—I think."

"Toby, you're doing the right thing. If you want to be anything on this team besides the twelfth man, Coach has to trust you. And if he can't trust you with his daughter, why would he trust you with the basketball?"

· 16 ·

Riding the bus to a game was nothing like riding the bus to a field trip. Everybody had a double seat of his own. Most of the guys were spread out. Some, like JJ, were in their own worlds, listening to music and staring out the window as the bus chugged past picnic areas overlooking the river, forest-fire warning signs, and boarded-up roadside gas stations. Another group was gathered around Ruben in the back of the bus for a card game.

Since the Cedar Crest game, one of the only guys besides Raj not giving me the cold shoulder was Malcolm. He was sitting with his back against a window; I was facing him with my back against the opposite window. Malcolm beamed as he held his warm-up shirt for me to see.

"Trashman?" I asked. "Your nickname is Trashman?"

"Because Trashman takes out the trash."

"You fool," Roy yelled from the back. "It says Trashman because you only play during garbage time."

At least he plays, I thought, already picturing what Vinny Pesto would do when he saw me on the end of the bench. Probably point to his stupid championship patch while jogging past me. Or when we lined up to shake hands after the game, would he get in my face and say "Once a gym rat, always a gym rat" or something lame like that?

We were in the visitors' locker room at Hamilton when McKlusky sat next to me. The way he exhaled, I could tell he was bent out of shape about something.

"I got your note," he said at last.

"What note?"

McKlusky handed me the note I had written earlier.

"McKlusky, this note wasn't for you."

"It wasn't?"

"No! It was for Megan. Who did you think M was?"

"Me."

"You! Why would I tell *you* you had a nice smile?"

"Actually, *pretty* nice smile is what you said."

"McKlusky! You never gave this note to Megan?"

JJ looked up from his locker. "Everything okay?"

McKlusky rolled his eyes as he walked away.

Raj appeared. "What was that all about?"

"McKlusky never gave Megan the note."

"So she still likes you?"

"Yeah." The situation was getting out of control.

Just then Coach Applewhite gathered us around the chalkboard, where he had sketched the outline of a basketball court. "The Hamilton Harriers are defending champions for a reason," he said. "They have a guard named Vinny Pesto who can step back and hurt us from the perimeter or put it on the floor and penetrate." Coach made a chalk mark near the top of the arc. "We also have to worry about the Landusky twins. Melvin and Marvin. Watch out. One of them is right-handed. The other is left-handed." Two marks appeared in the paint. "Now, remember what we talked about this week. Morelli—you're our best defender. Your job is to stick to Pesto. Now, as for the Landusky twins . . ."

Raj whispered to me, "I heard that when a mountain lion wandered into Tompkins Park last summer, the Landusky twins wrestled it to the ground and led it away with a jump rope and a dog collar."

"What were the Landusky twins doing at Tompkins Park with a jump rope and a dog collar?"

Raj shrugged. "All I know is what I heard."

Coach cleared his throat and looked at me and Raj. "Is everyone clear on what to do?"

We all nodded.

"Are there any questions?"

"What about offense?" Roy asked.

Coach checked his watch. "What *about* offense?"

"Is JJ going to take all the shots again?"

Everyone was silent.

"For Pete's sake, Morelli!" Coach barked at last.

"We've been through this before. We run the offense through JJ because he is our primary scoring threat. If the rest of you crash the boards and move without the ball, your shots will come off passes and misses."

"If he ever misses," Roy grumbled.

"That's exactly my point, Morelli. Remember what I said at the beginning of the season. This is about twelve people being a part of something bigger than any one person. If you have a problem with that, you need to ask yourself what you're doing on this team."

Coach gave us a moment to think about that before pulling us together for a pregame cheer.

"Come on, Chuckers!" Ruben said loudly. "We can do this! It's time to shock the world. No more losing. Shock the world!" When nobody spoke, Ruben said, *"Shock the world!"*

"Shock the world," we repeated. Nobody was sure how loudly to chant. We were chanting rookies.

We tried once more. Then Coach said it was time to take the court. I jumped up and down like a boxer. Even if Coach never put me in the game, I had to be ready for Vinny Pesto. I had promised him Pilchuck would be for real this season. It was time to start proving it.

The gym at Hamilton Middle School was called the Cage. The bleachers came right down to the court, leaving just enough room for the benches. With the low ceilings and bars over the windows, the room felt more like a prison yard than a place to play basketball. Or at least how I pictured a prison yard would look. We had just entered the gym when Coach stopped, snapped his fingers, pivoted, and, spying me, said, "Shoot. I forgot my clipboard in the locker room. Wheeler, do me a favor and grab it. And see if you can find a water bottle while you're at it."

At the moment, I was scanning the gym for Vinny Pesto, hoping that either he would not see me, or, if he did, that he would not realize he was seeing the last man on the bench. I was trying to look like I belonged by jogging slowly, not smiling, and basically doing anything possible to fit in with the others. So when Coach asked me to do an errand, he touched a nerve.

"Why me?" I asked.

Coach answered sharply. "Because I asked you to."

I lowered my head and spoke quietly. "Sorry, Coach."

"It's too late for sorry, son." He got right in my face. "Listen to me. Do you want to contribute to the success of this team?"

"Yes, sir."

"Then you better get used to one idea *right now*. Your attitude is your contribution. When I tell you to do something, you don't ask *why*, you do it. You got that?"

I nodded.

"Good. Now get back in that locker room and find my clipboard."

I saw what was happening. Coach might have said *find my clipboard*, but he was really saying *stay away from my daughter*. There was no doubt about it. He was punishing me. Obviously, Megan had come home from school yesterday with my jacket and Coach had discovered whose it was.

Coming back from the locker room, I came face to face with Vinny Pesto, who looked at the clipboard and water bottle in my hands and began laughing hysterically. It was my worst fear.

We were standing directly in front of the gigantic display case full of the trophies Hamilton athletic teams had won over the years. Front and center were the basketball trophies.

"I thought I saw you getting off the bus," Vinny said. Carefully, he wiped a tiny smudge from the glass. "Then I thought, *Nah, that couldn't be Toby the Gym Rat, not in an actual uniform.* But now it all makes sense—you couldn't play basketball, so they made you an equipment manager."

I was in no mood for his sorry trash talk. I breathed on the glass and was pleased to see a foggy spot stick. Then I drew an *L* in the smudge—for *loser.* "Are you finished, Pesto?" I asked. "I have somewhere to be."

Vinny used his jersey to clear the smudge. "Where—the bench?"

"I'll see you on the court, Vinny," I said with another breath on the glass.

We stared at each other. Neither of us wanted to leave the other alone in front of the trophy case. Finally, Raj poked his head into the hallway and said, "It's game time, Toby," and we moved slowly toward the court.

"You first," said Vinny, eyeing the glass.

"After you, Miss," I said.

Later, sitting in my seat during a disastrous first half, I felt as though the whole world was against me. All I wanted to do was wipe that smirk from Vinny's face—and a championship of our own was the only way to do it. But as long as my place on the bench was the basketball equivalent of Pluto, there was nothing I could do except keep my seat warm, fetch water bottles, and leave breath marks on Hamilton's trophy case.

Roy did his best to contain Pesto. He fought through screens, tried to cut off passes, and kept a hand in his face on jump shots. In the paint, our big men were no match for the Landusky twins. Coach Applewhite stood on the sideline, hollering for Khalil and Mc-Klusky to force Melvin and Marvin away from the basket, but it was no use. Hamilton was beating us inside and out. JJ had fifteen points, but it wasn't enough.

Coach called two time-outs in the fourth quarter. During the first time-out, he encouraged JJ to keep shooting. The others he comanded, "Move with or without the basketball! Find a way to get open. Use your screens. Make your cuts."

Megan was on the outer edge of the huddle. When Coach paused, she added, shouting over the crowd noise, "Try to force their big men to bring the ball upcourt—they might turn the ball over."

I'm not sure if Megan's speaking up ticked off some

of the guys because she was a girl, because she was Coach's daughter, or because we were losing, but her suggestion definitely stepped on some toes. And Roy let it be known. "What is she—a coach?" he said in earshot of Megan, Coach, and the whole team. "Why is she always around? Shouldn't she be with her own team?" I think Roy knew the girls' games were mostly on Wednesdays and Thursdays. Besides, that wasn't really the point.

Coach was starting to overheat. "For crying out loud, Morelli, this is not the time or the place to discuss this. You worry about what you have to do out there."

"I'm just sayin' what everyone's thinking."

Megan shrank away. It had never occurred to me to question her role. I just thought it was nice having her on the end of the bench.

A few minutes later, Coach called the second timeout. He had some things to say about the offense. "As long as JJ has nobody to pass to, the defense is going to keep coming at him with that double-team. I want you guys to *think*!"

"So it's *our* fault we're losing?" asked Roy, pointing to the scoreboard.

Coach exploded. He kicked the chair closest to his feet so hard, Raj had to jump to avoid being hit. *"Morelli!* You're finished! Pick up your stuff and get out of my sight. *Now!"*

Roy marched off, but not before getting in the last word. "Just so you know, there's more than one person on this team. And we're not in *college,* and we don't all just care about *winning!*"

Coach watched Roy leave. For a moment, he seemed lost. Rattled. Then he looked at the rest of us and got down to business. "We're going to stay in the box-and-one," he said. "McKlusky, you and Khalil have got to shut those big guys down. I don't care if you have to grow ten inches before the end of the time-out. Do you hear me? Raj, you stay on the perimeter. JJ, can you shut down that Pesto kid for the rest of the night?"

JJ said, "I can do it, Coach."

Coach took a deep breath. Did he know we needed a fifth player on the court? He became animated again as the buzzer blew. *"Who's mad?"* he yelled.

Nobody spoke. Coach was not just yelling. He was erupting.

"I'm mad!" Coach went on. "I'm so mad I want to break this chair in two. I want to put on a jersey and go out on that court and kick someone's butt myself! Unfortunately, they won't let me play in this game. That means someone else is going to have to go out there and do it. So who's mad?"

I was wide-eyed. So was everyone else. But I guess nobody wanted to be sent to the locker room, because there was no answer to the question. Instead, some guys looked at each other. A few just looked at their shoes. Coach slammed his clipboard to the floor and turned his back on us. When he turned to face us again, he sounded desperate. "Well, since the rest of you guys won't do it, and *I* have to stay here on the sideline, I guess we might as well try something new." Then he tugged me by the loose front of my jersey. "Wheeler, get your butt out there and do something."

I was too juiced to be nervous. Seeing Coach fired up in the fourth quarter of a game we were losing by nineteen points was like a shot of electricity. He could have sat back and let the clock run out; but he didn't. He was coaching like he still thought we could win. That was why I was too excited to think straight.

The buzzer blew and I ran directly onto the court.

JJ stopped me. "You have to check in," he said.

"Right," I said, feeling my face go beet red.

It was our ball. JJ dribbled upcourt. He passed the ball to Raj on the wing. I waited on the opposite wing with Khalil. Our only job was to spread out the court so the defense had no chance to help on JJ, which was fine with me. Sure, I wanted to score. But those first minutes on the court during an actual game were a blur. I had always thought that when Coach sent me into a game, I would pause to soak it in. Savor the moment. But everything happened so quickly that the sounds of the game were suddenly unfamiliar. When I sat on the bench, it was easy to pick up distinct voices. Now I was deaf. Even though I was just a few feet away, the voices all merged into one distant hum. Playing with a ref was strange too, and for the first time, I realized how far I was from the rec center.

The play unfolded cleanly. McKlusky came up from

the post to set a screen for JJ, who cut to the block. Raj dribbled around a second screen from McKlusky. With a third screen, JJ shed his man, took a pass from Raj, and lofted a jump shot that fell short. Marvin, the left-handed Landusky twin, snagged the rebound and flipped an outlet pass to a guard, and Hamilton pushed the ball upcourt, but not before we recovered and forced them into their half-court offense. I picked up the guy who had guarded me. JJ picked up Vinny and shadowed him from one wing, across the baseline, and up to the other wing, fighting through screens as he went.

I had sworn to Vinny we would be on the court together—and now we were. Of course, it was only the first step—I still had to hit the winning shot in his face at the end of the championship game. And even though it was kind of tough to trash-talk a guy I wasn't guarding, I couldn't let this moment pass without Pesto hearing from me. "You gotta deal with me now, Vinny. I'm here and I'm gonna be there at the end."

"Go back to the rec center, gym rat."

"You first, ch—"

"Toby!" JJ yelled. He was pointing to my man. I spun around to see that he had broken toward the corner, where Khalil was using every pound of his body to keep Melvin Landusky away from the basket. Suddenly Melvin set a screen for the guard and then rolled to the high post. But Khalil stayed near the low block. I raced to catch up with my man, leaving Melvin wide open on the elbow, where he caught a pass and nailed a short jumper.

I didn't think Coach could get any madder than he already was, but he did. As soon as he could, he sent Ruben back in and yanked me to the bench. "What did I say in the locker room?" he demanded. "About the box-and-one?"

My mind went blank. The only thing I remembered was Raj whispering something to me about the Landusky twins and a mountain lion.

Coach rubbed his forehead. "Wheeler, how the heck am I supposed to put you in the game if you don't even know what defense we're playing? You were supposed to be in a zone out there. Do you remember what a zone is?"

"Yeah, you guard an area instead of a man."

"Then how did that big fella get wide open in the middle of the court?"

"I thought we were playing man-to-man."

"Did you hear me when I explained the box-and-one before the game?"

"Um . . ." I glanced at my shoes.

"In a box-and-one, four of you are playing zone. But you followed your man. You weren't listening." Coach sighed. "Wheeler, I don't care where you sit on the bench. You have to be ready to play at all times. Otherwise, you're just taking up space. I didn't put you on the team just to take up space."

The game ended. I was mad at myself. I hadn't

single-handedly cost us the game, but I had screwed up. Again. And this time I had screwed up in front of Vinny Pesto. As it turned out, I wasn't the only person upset. When we were sitting in silence in the locker room later, Ruben slammed his fist into a locker, denting it.

Mellowing after his tirades on the court, Coach said, "Ruben, part of competition is learning to lose."

"I don't want to learn how to *lose*," Ruben fired back. "I want the rest of these guys to learn how to *win*. I'm sick of losing. We're better than this."

"I'm glad to hear it," said Coach. He loosened his tie and pushed a stray hair back into place.

Ruben turned to us. "We've got two weeks off now. We're 0 and 3 with seven games left. One more loss and we're done and it's another year without a championship for Pilchuck."

Coach nodded at Ruben, then slipped out the door, leaving us alone.

Ruben stood on a bench. "We gotta start playing like a team. We aren't helping each other on defense. We're not talking on the court. The only noise I hear is about who took how many shots. That ends tonight," he said, looking at Roy. "I don't care whether you're a captain, a general, or the twelfth man. The next game is the start of a new season for everybody. From now on, we play as a team, and we win as a team."

I looked around the gym. I was surprised to see JJ nodding along with Ruben and clapping quietly—almost to himself. Other guys were doing the same thing.

There were no more hanging heads. Soon everyone was clapping.

Raj shouted, "Let's do it, Chuckers!"

"Let's win, baby," added Trashman.

"One more thing," Ruben said. "We're gonna see these guys again. And next time, we're gonna win."

· 17 ·

We gathered in the hallway outside the locker room. In a minute, we would be boarding the bus back to Pilchuck. Tempers had cooled. Most of the team and some of the fans were planning to go for pizza when we got home. I had already cleared it with my parents. When Megan heard that, she went up to Coach. I watched as she asked, then begged to go.

"You are so overbearing," Megan said. "Why do you have to know where I am *all* the time?"

"Because I'm your father and that's my job."

"We're just going for pizza, Dad."

"That's how it starts," Coach answered, nodding.

But Megan refused to give up. Coach pulled her farther away from the group, probably to explain some new Dr. Barb special he had seen about what happened to girls who ate pizza after basketball games. Then I guessed he asked Megan, "Who else is going?"

Megan pointed to Valerie.

"Anyone else?"

She looked over her shoulder. And pointed at me!

I tried to duck behind McKlusky. But Coach had tracked Megan's finger and had spied me easily. I waved, trying to look innocent. Before Coach could come after me, though, Mrs. Applewhite appeared with his coat. Megan explained the situation. Her mom nodded, overruling Coach. "Be home by eleven," she said.

"Ten-forty-five," Coach said.

"I will," Megan promised.

She ran over to me. "Ready?" she asked.

Seeing that Coach was gone, I relaxed and said, "I am now."

We boarded the bus and took our seats. Megan sat in front with Valerie. I found a seat to myself halfway back. As the bus rolled along the highway, winding with the river below, I replayed my first minutes of game time. Okay, so I wasn't an all-star yet. But I had been on the court, wearing a uniform, in front of real fans. I'd come a long way for a gym rat. And even though I missed the action at the rec center, after a taste of a *real* game, I wanted more.

The bus was turning onto Verlot Street when JJ sat down next to me. "Hey, man," he said, surprising me. How long had it been since he had started a conversation?

Weeks at least. "Do you think it'd be cool with your folks if I crashed at your place tonight?"

"Is your dad out of town?"

"No. That's the problem. He's waiting for me with a videotape of the game. I already know I went 0 for 50. I don't need him to remind me."

That made me think about what Roy had said earlier—that this wasn't college and that winning wasn't everything. College was big bucks and big crowds and superstars on television. And tons of pressure to win. Eighth grade wasn't supposed to be like that. But we did have a star and we did play to win. I wondered who was right, Roy or Ruben—or Coach. Would I rather sit on the bench and cheer the guys who gave us the best chance to win—or play my fair share of minutes even if it meant we might not be as competitive? If we kept losing, it wouldn't matter. One thing was sure, JJ didn't make being the star seem like very much fun—to judge by the look on his face. It wasn't quite desperation, but it was close.

I took my time answering him, because I wasn't sure how to feel about all this. I didn't know whether to be happy because JJ wanted to hang out at my house— something he hadn't done since before summer—or to be suspicious that he was only doing it to avoid a lecture from his dad. And then I decided that this was what friends were for—to forgive and to help each other. So I held out my hand and said, "Sure. It'd be cool."

JJ slapped my hand. "Thanks, buddy."
Buddy?

Corner Pizza was packed. JJ and I elbowed our way to the back. Megan sat in a booth with Valerie. JJ sat next to Valerie, who saw me and said, "You. Over there. Where I can see you."

Lucky for her, nature was calling.

I was in a pretty good mood as I made my way to the men's room. We had lost, but I *had* played. JJ was coming over later. And there was an extra-large pepperoni pizza on the way. What could go wrong?

And then I came back from the bathroom.

McKlusky was standing next to the booth. He was talking to Megan. She seemed confused, like he was speaking Japanese. Of course, she was in the middle of a conversation with McKlusky, so that made sense. Then I watched in gut-splitting horror as McKlusky reached into his coat pocket and pulled out a folded-up note.

It all went down in slow motion.

I tried to push my way to the table, but there were too many bodies. Yelling was no use either. The jukebox was too loud. Megan unfolded the note. She squinted. Her forehead crinkled. Her nose twitched. She was refolding the paper just as I reached the table.

"Is this a joke?" she asked.

"I . . ."

"Can we just be *friends*?" She stood and gathered her bags. "What did you think we were?"

All I could do was stammer, "Y-you borrowed m-my jacket."

Megan was seething. "Toby, if you think your biggest problem on the team is being friends with the coach's daughter, you're even more clueless than I thought."

Then she was gone.

When I was sitting again, Valerie put the note in front of me. "A *pretty* nice smile? Seriously, Toby, even I would say something nicer than that."

"I guess there's a first time for everything."

I was joking, but there was nothing funny about what had happened. "I don't get it. What did I do that was so wrong?"

Sounding disgusted, Valerie asked, "Toby, do you know anything about girls?"

"No," I said, sinking in my seat. "I don't. I really, really don't."

"I'm only going to tell you this because Megan is my friend and because you clearly need help. You did three things wrong." Valerie raised one finger. "You made it seem like you were choosing basketball over being friends with her, which is bad." Then she raised another. "And you acted like there was more going on than there really was, which is even worse. Girls do not like being told when we're more than just friends with someone.

Also, you did it with a note, which is the dumbest idea in the world."

Amazing. Valerie had nailed it. In thirty seconds, she had broken down the entire mess and put me in my place. I didn't know anybody else, except my parents, who had the guts to be so honest with me. Maybe that was what JJ liked about Valerie. She was the only person not telling him how great he was—or how much better he needed to be.

"So I'm a jerk?" I asked.

"A huge jerk."

"Should I go after her?"

"Being a jerk is bad enough. Don't be a stalker, too."

"What *should* I do?"

Valerie pulled out her mirror. "I don't know," she said. "Have you tried being her friend? She's always telling me how nobody goes to the girls' games. Maybe you should go to one."

JJ came back to the table with Stephen, who high-fived me. JJ placed the large pizza on the table.

When the pizza was almost gone, I said to JJ, "We can call my dad for a ride home now if you want."

"It's only ten o'clock," said JJ. "What did you want to do, go trick-or-treating?"

The table was silent.

When I was in third grade, my hand got slammed in a car door, leaving me with two broken fingers. The pain was unbearable. This was a different kind of pain, but it hurt all the same.

When JJ had blown me off on Halloween (foul one), I'd gotten over it. When he'd skipped out on hoops (foul two), I'd gotten over that, too. But now he had gone out of his way to make me feel lower than dirt in front of his friends. It was definitely JJ's third personal foul. And a flagrant one, too. In an NBA game that would be two shots and possession—and a fine from the commissioner. My only hope was to not let them see that it bothered me. So I kept it together and said, "Yeah—like anyone would have candy in November."

"Anyway," JJ said, "we're gonna hang out for a while. You can stay if you want. But if you go, will you leave your window open for me? I'll be in late."

That did it.

Another flagrant foul: making fun of me in front of his friends *and* attempting the combo blow off/sleepover *on the same possession.*

"Leave a window open?" I shouted. "*Leave a window open?* I'll leave a window open for you, jerk. I'll leave it open and then I'll close it on your guitar-picking fingers."

"Whoa, relax," said Stephen.

But I had nothing more to say.

JJ tried to stop me as I walked out of Corner Pizza. "Toby, come on. I was just kidding. I'll come with you now. I shouldn't have said that. Where am I supposed to sleep tonight?"

"Not my problem," I said without looking back.

JJ had stood me up, blown me off, ditched me, and made me feel like a chump for the last time. He'd better hope he never needed me for anything again, because, as far as I was concerned, he had just fouled out of the game.

· 18 ·

The next week was overcast. Megan wouldn't talk to me at school. Whenever I tried to get her attention in the hallway or the cafeteria, she would turn her head back toward her friends on the basketball team or whoever else she had been talking to. It must have been something in the rain causing grudges to spread. After all, I was giving JJ the cold shoulder the same as Megan was giving it to me. The feeling he'd left me with after that night at Corner Pizza was like a week-long sucker punch. It wasn't that he had wanted to come over just to avoid his dad that bothered me. It was that even when he needed me, he *still* found a way to make me feel like a kid. The only good thing was that I had stood up for myself. All I wanted to do now was get better at basketball, help my team win, and maybe get in another game.

We had no games the week of Thanksgiving, and we

wouldn't have one again until the first week of December. That meant two Fridays in a row without a game. So we practiced, practiced, practiced. And ran, ran, ran. After my appearance in the Hamilton game, it was back to the end of the bench for me. And if being the twelfth man was bad before I had gotten to play, it was 100 percent *awful* after the fact. Even worse, Coach was singling me out more than ever. During a scrimmage just before Thanksgiving, I took a jump shot and watched proudly as it hit nothing but net.

"Wheeler," Coach said as he marched over to me, squinting. "What the heck was that?"

Roy put his hands on his knees. "Here we go again."

"What was what, Coach?"

"Take another jump shot," he ordered.

Raj flipped the ball to me. I shot again. This time it went off the side of the rim.

Coach crossed his arms. He stood close to me and spoke quietly. "Why are you shooting from your shoulder?"

"That's how I've always shot."

"Nobody's ever taught you how to shoot?" he asked.

I shook my head. "I've never had a coach."

Coach rubbed his forehead. There was something different in the way he was speaking to me. I hadn't known his voice could drop below a holler. But now his tone was hushed and even considerate, like a doctor trying to figure out what was wrong with his patient. Part of me enjoyed the attention, but as the rest of the team looked on, another part of me wished he would just tell me what I had done wrong and be done with it.

"Wheeler, I want you to meet me here in the gym. Saturday morning. Okay?"

I shuffled my feet. "Sure, Coach. I'll be there. I mean here."

At the sound of the whistle, the scrimmage started again. I stayed on the court, but I played poorly. I was distracted. Why did Coach want to see me in the gym? Had I done something wrong? Was this even about basketball? After three more minutes, Coach sent me to the sideline. I sat on the bench, put my chin in my hands, and waited for more wind sprints.

At least Dad had something to be thankful for. Earlier that week he had come home all smiles and announced that Warren Goodman wanted to see him *right after the holiday* to discuss the promotion. I had never seen Dad that happy. Mom was less enthusiastic.

Over Thanksgiving dinner, she said, "I just think it's odd that after all these months, Warren is suddenly interested in your promotion."

"Maybe he thinks I deserve it," Dad replied.

"You do deserve it," Mom said. "Eat some peas," she said to me.

Dad scooped a spoonful of potatoes onto his plate. "You think Warren is buttering me up to get you to lay off Landover?"

"Isn't it possible?"

Dad momentarily lost interest in his food. "Even if it was true, why would Warren think I could do anything? I have no control over what you or the Cascade Group does."

They were quiet for a moment. "He is a little dense," I added, repeating something Dad had said a hundred times.

Taking a bite of stuffing, Dad declared, "That's all right, Toby. I'm not going to be a wood chip salesman for the rest of my life. My lightbulb moment will come."

"What's a lightbulb moment?" I asked.

Dad tapped his forehead. "The million-dollar idea, Toby. I was watching a show on television. It's called *Dr. Barb* . . ."

Here we go again.

But Dad continued, ". . . and Dr. Barb says everyone has at least one million-dollar idea in his lifetime. The trick is knowing when it comes."

"Do you feel one coming?" I asked.

"I hope so," he said cheerfully. "Warren told me when we sit down he wants to hear my ideas for increasing profits. I've been racking my brain for something that'll knock his socks off. But I haven't come up with anything yet."

Dad and I cleared the table. When Mom was done stacking plates, she said, "Well, while we wait for your lightbulb moment, how about some pie?"

When the pie was out of the oven, Dad suggested we say what we were thankful for.

Mom said she was thankful for her family. And for what remained of our old-growth forests.

Dad said he was thankful for his family. And for his job at Landover Lumber, even if he was just a wood chip salesman.

"What about you, Toby?" Mom asked.

"Well, I'm thankful for my family, I guess. And . . . um . . . I guess that's it."

"Just us?" Dad asked. "What about the basketball team? Aren't you thankful for that gift? After all, you're one of the twelve best basketball players in the school."

Even though I had never thought about it quite like that, I still said, "Sometimes I think I should have stayed at the rec center."

Mom looked me in the eye. "We're very proud of you for taking the chance you took, but you may not walk away without seeing the job through."

"What job?" I asked. "All I do is keep a seat warm."

Dad put down his fork. His voice was testy. "Toby," he said. "Enough. I don't want to hear another complaint about your role on the team. I don't care if you're a superstar or a benchwarmer, it's like your mother said—you figure out what your job is and you do it the best you can."

I wondered if he was talking about me—or himself.

But I got the message. Every day, Dad went to work

to do a job he thought he was too good for. He vented sometimes, but mostly he did the best he could do and waited for his chance. If our life was a basketball game, then Mom was the one who would keep fighting until the buzzer blew, even if there was no chance of winning. That was how they were. So how had I become a quitter and a pouter? I wasn't sure, but suddenly I saw it. And I didn't like it.

The next day, Friday, Raj invited me to play Risk with him and McKlusky. He said his cousin would be there too. *Good,* I thought. *I have a few things to say to the doctor of love. Like that his note-writing idea needs some serious rethinking.*

I rode my bike to Raj's house—the first time since the end of summer I had taken it out of the garage. JJ and I used to ride everywhere—until he decided it was cooler to walk or skateboard. As the sun sparkled off the snow on the mountains, I pedaled along the river, enjoying the brisk breeze and not caring what anyone thought.

Raj met me at the door and showed me to his basement, where a Risk board—a world map—was set up on a card table. The room was cozy. Thick carpet. A dartboard on the wall. And a minifridge in the corner. Two people were sitting at the table snacking on chips and pretzels. One of the people was McKlusky. The other person was Superman. At least someone dressed like Superman. The cape, the red tights tucked into the boots, and a blue shirt with a red *S* on the chest.

"Toby," said Raj. "This is my cousin—Sami."

"*This* is your cousin?" I asked. "The one with the three girlfriends?"

"Two, actually," Sami corrected me. "Heidi wasn't my type." He adjusted his cape. "By the way, how did things work out with that girl?"

"How did things work out with that girl? I'll tell you how things worked out with that girl. She called me clueless. Now she won't return my calls."

"Did you try writing a note?" Sami asked.

I ignored his question and instead pointed to a box of stuff at our feet. Inside were a baseball cap, a boomerang, one of those furry Russian hats, and a coffee can. "What's all that for?" I asked.

Raj explained, "The object of the game is to conquer continents. So whenever you conquer a continent, you get one of the items from the box."

"If you take over Europe, you wear the beret," McKlusky said.

Sami held up the boomerang. "This is for Australia."

I looked around the table. At McKlusky with his red curly hair stuffed into a black beret. At Raj, holding a plastic elephant. And at Sami, the ladies' man. They looked back at me. "Sounds good to me," I said, scooping up the dice. "But one thing I don't understand: Why is he dressed like Superman?"

"My Batman outfit is in the wash," Sami explained matter-of-factly.

As Raj, Sami, McKlusky, and I divided the globe among ourselves, we talked about the Winter Blast. Raj and McKlusky were still getting their courage up to ask Cassandra and Melanie.

"What you need to do," Sami began, "is let the girls know that you see them as more than dates. The secret is to show them you think they're interesting people."

"They are interesting people," McKlusky said as he took over Peru.

Sami rolled the dice and moved his armies into Western Europe. "What do you know about them?"

"They're in my math class," I said.

Sami was unimpressed. "Anything else?"

"Basketball," Raj said. "They play basketball."

Sami was silent. He seemed to be processing the new information. While he meditated, I rubbed my hands and took my turn. I felt comfortable in Raj's basement. Even after McKlusky countered my attack on Yakutsk and sent me reeling back into Mongolia, I was laughing, enjoying myself. Raj and McKlusky never made me wonder if there was something wrong with me. They were fine being themselves, and—around them—I was fine being myself too.

After a trip to the bathroom, Sami spoke again. "I have one word for you," he said to Raj and McKlusky.

"What?" asked Raj.

Sami leaned back in his chair. "Limousine."

"A limo?" Raj asked. He wasn't sold. "Will that work?"

"The girls are on the basketball team, right?" Sami said. "Well, one day next week, have the limo waiting outside the gym. When practice is over, they'll come out and see the car and driver. Then you two step out with flowers and offer them a ride home."

"In their sweaty clothes?" McKlusky asked.

"I don't know if the driver is going to go for that," Raj agreed.

Sami cracked open a soda. "Will you relax? The driver won't care if you tip him ahead of time."

McKlusky scratched his head. "How much is this going to cost?"

"A hundred. Maybe two hundred. Depending on how long."

McKlusky opened his wallet. "I've got a buck."

"I don't know about this," Raj said.

"Trust me," Sami assured them. "This will work."

Raj turned to me. "Toby, what do you think?"

What did I think? I thought unless there was a fleet of limos rolling around Pilchuck looking for a bunch of sweaty eighth graders needing a lift home, they could take Sami's plan and flush it down the toilet right that minute. Not that I had any better ideas. Then I remembered what Valerie had said to me when I asked her how to get Megan to speak to me again.

"Why don't you just go to one of their games and ask them afterward? If they've won, they'll be in a good mood. If they've lost, you'll probably make their day."

"If you do it my way," Sami countered, "you get to ride home in a car with a TV and a stereo."

Raj looked back and forth. "That would be nice. On the other hand, Cassandra did ask me to come to one of her games."

I pointed to McKlusky's wallet. "And my way is free."

"Toby wins!" McKlusky said.

Raj agreed free was better than two hundred bucks for a ride home. Sami said the least they could do was bring the flowers. After that, we went back to the game. The hours passed quickly. Before I knew it, I was wearing an oversized fur hat, clutching a boomerang, and saying things like "Ukraine is mine!" Raj forgot all about the dance and I forgot all about JJ and all about Megan. It was only when I got home that night and saw my basketball shoes that I remembered I was supposed to meet Coach at school the next day. Was I going to basketball detention? Or getting a private lesson?

· 19 ·

The next morning, Coach met me at the front door of school. He was dressed in gray pants and a green sweater. We walked down the empty hallway to the gym office. When we were seated across from each other, he looked me in the eye and asked, "Toby, did you think I was punishing you because you were spending time with my daughter?"

I felt like a dope. "Sort of. Yes, sir."

He put his elbows on his desk and laced his hands so that both pointer fingers were aimed at me like a gun. "You should know that decisions I make about basketball have nothing to do with Megan," he began. "I put you on the roster because I saw something that day at the rec center. And I put you on the bench because you needed to develop as a basketball player. I did the same thing a hundred times with college walk-ons. When I see a kid with talent and heart, I give him a chance. Sometimes the experiment pays off, sometimes it doesn't. You have a chance to be one of the good ones, Wheeler, but only if you're willing to work on every aspect of your game."

I was eager to show him how hard I could work and relieved to be back on his good side. "I am, Coach," I promised. "And I'm sorry if I hurt Megan's feelings."

He tapped the framed picture next to his clipboard. "The fact that Megan reacted the way she did only means she cares about what you think. She's a tough kid, but she bruises."

She bruises? Coach has been watching too much Dr. Barb, I thought. "The point is, I can't protect her forever, no matter how much I'd like to." Coach looked up at the wall like an actor trying to remember his next line. "So I promised not to hover over her like an overbearing spy every time she's around a boy." He cleared his throat, then said, "You're probably wondering why I asked you to come in this morning."

"Is it my two-handed jumper?"

"That's part of it," Coach replied. "Look, this is my first year with this team too. I've had to make a lot of adjustments. Sometimes I forget you guys aren't playing for a trip to the Final Four. Or that you're still learning." He picked up a pencil and began tapping it on his desk. "What I'm trying to say here is that *I'm* still learning—

just like you. Anyway, the other night I realized I needed to make some changes."

"So Roy was right?" I asked.

Coach gripped the pencil tightly. I thought he might snap it. "In his own way, yeah, Morelli was right."

First all that business about Megan's feelings and now *Morelli was right*? I wondered if Coach was going soft. "What does this have to do with me, Coach?"

"What do I always say about this team, Toby?"

" 'Do it again'?"

Coach shook his head. "It takes twelve of you to win. And I need you to be ready to play—just in case. I thought you could use a private lesson to catch up."

"Like tutoring?" I asked.

Coach nodded. "Like tutoring." Suddenly, we heard footsteps outside the office. The door began to open. Coach smiled. "And here's your tutor now," he said as Megan walked in.

At first I thought Coach was joking. But nobody was laughing.

"Hey, look," I said as I followed her out of the office. "I'm really sorry about the note and everything. I got some bad advice from someone who turned out to not exactly be the world's leading expert on this stuff. And not to blame the victim or anything, but you *were* the one who said your dad was a little paranoid, so I guess you could say we're both at fault. Anyway, I'm ready to bury the hatchet if you are."

When we got to the gym, I saw there was a line of cones down the middle of the court spread a few feet apart. Megan still had not responded to my apology. Instead, she walked to the sideline and pulled something from her pocket.

Suddenly the silence of the gym was shattered by the shriek of a whistle. Startled, I jumped high enough to dunk. "What'd you do that for?"

Megan let the whistle fall around her neck. "Practice is in session."

"Where's Coach?" I asked.

"He's in his office. Doing paperwork. Today I'm your coach."

Oh, great. A coach with a score to settle, and a whistle—a bad combination.

We began with a game called Around the World. Megan said it was a shooting drill, which sounded fine to me until I realized she was lying. The goal of Around the World was to make it around the perimeter of the paint without missing. Megan handed me the basketball and told me to start on the left low-block—just two feet from the basket. I banked in a shot, then tried a shot from four feet. Easy enough, right? *Clank.* I missed.

Megan blew the whistle again. "Down and back once!"

"Down and back where?"

"To the other end of the gym and back, gym rat. Run!"

"You can't make me run. Who do you think—"

Megan blew the whistle, more loudly this time.

I ran.

When I was done running, Megan told me to start over. "This time," she said, "try shooting with one hand."

"Why?"

"Because your form is atrocious, that's why. When you shoot, only your strong hand should be behind the ball. The other hand should be on the side of the ball, guiding it, but barely touching it. For the close shots, just practice flicking the wrist on your shooting hand. We'll add the other hand for the longer shots."

It took ten tries, but eventually I made it around the world without missing. Shooting with one hand behind the ball felt weird at first, but after six or seven sprints to the end of the gym and back, I was open to anything.

"Next up," said Megan, "dribbling."

"I know how to dribble."

"Like you knew how to shoot?"

"At least I know how to subtract negative numbers."

Megan blew the whistle. "Down and back!"

"I didn't do anything!"

"You insulted the coach. Run!"

"*You* run."

Megan blew the whistle, more loudly still.

I ran.

Five minutes later, I was weaving between the cones, dribbling as I went from one end of the court to the other. "That wasn't so hard," I said.

"Do it again," said Megan. "This time watch my hands. When I say 'How many?' you tell me how many fingers I'm holding up."

"If I keep looking up, how am I supposed to see the ball?"

Megan huffed. "The point is to dribble with your hands, not your eyes. How do you think good guards find open men? Not by looking at their shoes . . . duh."

I had dribbled between one pair of cones when Megan called, "How many?"

Looking up, I saw she had raised three fingers. "Three," I yelled as the ball went off my foot.

The whistle blew. Down and back.

"Dribble with your fingertips," Megan said. "And keep the ball closer to your body."

More dribbling. More cones. More fingers. More running.

"Trust your hands!" Megan yelled.

I dribbled without looking down.

"Good," said Megan. "Now do it with your left hand."

We kept this up all day. We worked on shooting. We worked on passing. We worked on rebounds. Megan even rolled out a television and made me watch a movie about the motion offense. When I asked her if she had any popcorn, she blew the whistle and said, "Run!"

By the afternoon, I was looking forward to being back with Coach.

When Megan was satisfied with my progress, we sat side by side on the bleachers, staring in silence at the basketball court. I took the fact that she was sitting near me to mean that all was forgiven. I sure hoped so. I was too tired to run any more wind sprints.

· 20 ·

Even though we had been practicing all day, Megan and I decided to race down to the rec center to catch the last half hour of open gym. Plus, she said there was someone she thought I should talk to. When I pestered her to tell me who, she just said, "You'll see."

On the way there, she mentioned that Raj and McKlusky were going to the girls' game later in the week—she had heard the news from Cassandra and Melanie. "Are they going to ask them to the Winter Blast?" she asked.

"They're going to try," I said, although who knew if Raj and McKlusky could seal the deal on their first attempt?

"When?" Megan asked as we walked along Verlot Street.

"After one of your basketball games."

Megan turned to me. "You should come too, Toby. We're playing really well. But we need more fans."

"Sure, I'll come," I said, excited about the invitation.

We were standing on the corner, waiting for the light.

Megan shifted her bag. "So, um, are *you* going to ask anyone? To the Blast?"

"I can't dance," I said, both because it was true and because it was easier than explaining the truth, which was that if I was going to ask anyone it would be her, but only if someone gave me a shot of courage.

"You couldn't dribble with your left hand, either," she said. "Compared to that, dancing is easy."

"I'll think about it," I promised.

She nodded. "By the way, I don't think I'm going to sit on the bench anymore," she said.

"What—why not? You mean because of what Roy said?"

"They don't want me there. I'm not helping. I should just sit in the stands. It'll be better for everyone that way."

"Not me!"

Megan stood still and looked me in the eye. "Really?" she asked.

"Really," I repeated. "You just have to make yourself valuable."

"Look who's talking," Megan replied.

"Hey—I put up with your tutoring, didn't I?" I was joking, but I had to admit, Megan had a point.

As we pushed open the doors of the rec center, I felt like I was going back to a classroom I had left behind years ago. There were good memories, but everything seemed a half size too small.

Megan went to the office to call her mom. I went to the basketball court. The gym was quiet. No full-court action. Just a mellow game of three-on-three and a few people standing around talking. I was scanning the gym searching for whoever Megan had brought me here to see when, from the sideline, I heard someone say, "What's the matter, gym rat, did your team finally realize what a scrub you are? Or did Coach Applesauce send you for water again?"

I looked over and saw Vinny Pesto. "It's *Applewhite*, you pinhead."

Vinny strutted up to me. "I saw the standings the other day. Looks like Pilchuck is in the basement—again."

"So we're off to a slow start."

"You're 0 and 3, scrub," Vinny reminded me. He ran his hand through his porcupine hair. "Why don't you just accept it? Pilchuck isn't even going to make the play-offs. You're not going to be in the championship game and *nobody* is hitting any game-winning shot in my face."

"We're gonna win, Pesto. And I'm gonna be there."

"Then what are you doing back here?" he asked. "Is the benchwarmer not getting much PT?"

I had to give it to Vinny. The guy knew which

buttons to push. Even worse, I choked on the come-back. "It takes twelve guys to win one game," I said.

Vinny turned away, laughing. "Spoken like a true benchwarmer."

"I'll see you in January, chump!" I called after him.

A moment later, Megan appeared. "What did you promise this time?"

"Nothing new," I said. "So where's this mystery man?"

Megan looked around, then pointed. At the far end of the court, shooting free throws by himself, was a tall man wearing two knee braces and purple shorts.

Old Dude.

"That's who we came to see?" I whispered to Megan. "Old Dude?"

Megan gave me her patented *I can't believe I have to explain this to you* look and said, "His name is not *Old Dude,* Toby. It's Dr. Dinkins. And he happens to be a basketball legend."

"Never heard of him. Did he play in the NBA?"

"No."

"Overseas?"

"No."

"Where did he go to college?"

"Milton College."

"Where's that?"

"It doesn't exist anymore."

"Was he any good?"

"Hardly."

"Was the team any good?"

"Terrible."

"This is your big idea? To bring me to talk to a guy who never played except on a lousy team at a school that doesn't even exist?"

Old Dude—I mean Dr. Dinkins—saw us and waved. "Hello, Megan," he said. "How's your season going?"

"We've got a good team. We're even starting to get some crowds," said Megan. "Dr. Dinkins, you remember Toby Wheeler. From open gym?"

Old Dude—Megan could call him the King of Pilchuck for all I cared, he'd always be Old Dude to me—nodded and said, "You haven't been around much, Toby."

"Toby is on the school team," Megan explained.

"Barely," I added. "I'm the twelfth man. If I were any farther down the bench, I'd be in the snack stand selling hot dogs."

Old Dude snapped the basketball to me. "So you're a fellow pinerider?"

"A what rider?"

"Pine," Old Dude said. "Pinerider is another word for benchwarmer. But it means much more, if you ask me."

"You were on the bench?" I asked.

"If I'd been any farther down the bench, I would have been in the parking lot giving directions to the highway."

"But you played in college. Being a benchwarmer in

college is as good as being a starter in high school. It means you could play—right?"

"Let me tell you something about Milton College. Back then, there were fewer than two thousand students in the whole school, so we were in the lowest division. The basement. We played in the worst conference in the country, too. And in my first three years, we never finished better than last place."

"Let me get this straight. For three years, you were the worst player, on the worst team, in the worst conference, in the worst division in the country?"

Old Dude nodded. "I was the worst college basketball player in America."

"Tell him about your senior year," Megan said.

"After three years of sitting on the bench, I was ready to throw in the towel. But the day I went into the coach's office to quit, he told me about Landon Doozie."

"Doozie was his real name? Come on."

"Not only that—Landon Doozie was the most promising freshman ever recruited to play at Milton. Coach thought Doozie could turn the whole program around—put him and the school on the map. There was just one problem. Landon Doozie was what you might call a head case. Terrible grades. Couldn't get to practice on time to save his life. Disappeared for days without a word. But when he got on the court, he was unstoppable. Anyway, Coach asked me to stick around as a mentor. To keep the kid in line. For some reason, Doozie listened to me."

"So what happened?"

"Coach got his wish. Landon Doozie turned the program around overnight. Took us straight to the conference championship game."

"Did you get to play a lot that season?"

"Four minutes," said Old Dude. "In the last game of the regular season. We were up by thirty. Coach leaned down the bench and said, 'Dinkins, get in there.' "

"Did you score?"

"I did a lot more than that. In four minutes, I took seven shots, made two of them, added a free throw, blocked a shot, grabbed two rebounds, turned the ball over three times, and bloodied my lip diving for a loose ball."

"But your team was up by thirty!"

"When you're a pinerider, Toby, you play every second like it's your last. Every minute to you or me is like a full game to a starter. Our time is that much more precious."

"What happened in the championship game?"

"It was close in the beginning. We couldn't shake the other team. Their leading scorer, McAllister, was all over Landon, trying to provoke him, but Landon kept his cool. Then in the second quarter, McAllister and Doozie went chest to chest over a bump. I stood up to get Doozie's attention. That's when McAllister turns to me and says, 'Back off.' Well, the ref had had enough. He teed up McAllister not once but twice. And just like that the other guys had lost their star player. We cruised the rest of the way. Best year of my life."

"But you only got to play four minutes."

"True. On the other hand, without me, who knows, maybe Doozie would have done something foolish along the way and messed up the season for all of us. Or if McAllister had gotten the best of him in that game, maybe we would have ended up losing. The point is, Toby, I found a way to make a difference without ever touching the ball."

"It sounds good when you put it like that, but most of the time it feels like I don't even exist on the team."

"Do you know what the secret of being the twelfth man is?"

"No."

"You're the one guy on the team the fans really relate to. They see someone like Doozie and they see someone they wish they could be. But they see someone like you or me and they see someone they *know* they could be. We're human. That's why the benchwarmer is always a crowd favorite. The crowd wants to see him do well because they see him as one of their own. So your job is to get out there and give them something to cheer about. That's what separates the pineriders from the bench-warmers. We know our role. We do it well. And when push comes to shove, we rise to the occasion. You're a pinerider, Toby. When your time comes, be ready."

Monday was a good day for Mom and a bad day for Dad. The local paper had run a front-page feature on Sunday about Butte Peak and the Landover Lumber Company. Mom wasn't quoted or anything, but I knew she had been trying to get the story in print for a while. The article described how clear-cuts affected streams and rivers. There were diagrams and everything. The article made me pretty convinced the clear-cut was a bad idea, until I came home from practice and saw Dad slumped on the couch, his shirt untucked and his tie undone. Mom was sitting next to him. She was holding his hand. They were speaking softly. I could hear her apologizing, which surprised me. I had been thinking of this as a competition, like me and Pesto in a pickup game. But here was Mom, the winner, consoling Dad. I tried to picture Pesto apologizing to me after a game. And then I realized that what I was seeing between Mom and Dad was not about winning and losing. It was about family. At the end of the day, they were on the same team. And nothing that could happen to the south slope of Butte Peak would change that.

"Hi there," said Mom when she saw me.

"What's going on?" I asked.

"Warren Goodman spoke to Dad today," Mom

explained before going to the kitchen. "Well, he and some higher-ups from his office did."

"The article caused quite a stir at the office," Dad explained.

"I hope you didn't get the promotion, Dad, because if this is your happy face, you need help."

Dad sat up straight and rubbed his chin. "No promotion," he said slowly. Then he did his impression of a lumber company executive. "Warren said, 'Phil, if it was up to me . . . ,' then gave me some you-know-what about tight budgets and maybe next quarter. Blah, blah, blah."

"Is this all because of the article?" I asked.

"It's a big part of it," Dad sighed. "If the public is more sympathetic to the salmon, it isn't good for business. We lose money, people lose their jobs. And your old man doesn't get promoted."

Dad seemed pretty discouraged. I knew how he felt. "Hey, it's like you told me at Thanksgiving," I said, trying to remember his speech. "You may not like your job, but you go out and do it the best you can. I mean, my first choice wasn't to sit on the bench, but at least I'm *on* the team. Only twelve guys in the school can say that."

Dad squeezed my hand. "Thanks, Toby. But it's a little more complicated than that."

"Why? You know what they say in basketball—just take it straight to the hoop."

"Straight to the hoop," Dad repeated. "Straight to

the hoop." He stood up, muttering to himself. He snapped his fingers, then walked over to the desk in the hallway. He found a pencil and a piece of paper. "This could work," he said as he began punching numbers on a calculator.

"What could work?" I asked. "Something for your boss?"

Dad answered without looking up. "I'm not sure."

I got the idea that he was too distracted to explain.

After a few minutes of watching Dad's fingers fly on the calculator, I stretched and started to leave the room. I was sure we'd be smelling whatever Dad had cooking before too long.

· 21 ·

In the days leading up to our next game, we could all feel something different in the air. Everybody was running a little harder in practice, talking more during scrimmages, and complaining less about playing time.

Coach told us to think of it as another chance to start the season. Except we were 0–3 with seven games left. Finishing 7–3 might get us into the postseason league tournament. Or it might not. As for me and JJ, we were on the same team, but we were no longer best friends. Sometimes I thought I saw him watching me when I was joking around with Raj or McKlusky or one of the other guys. But if he had something to say to me, he never said it. He just did his thing quietly and let his basketball do the talking.

One day in practice, Coach was in a foul mood. Everything anyone did was wrong. We ran all afternoon while he stood on the sideline scowling. Even Roy seemed to know to keep his mouth shut. We were still running at 4:45, when Megan came into the gym, took a seat in the bleachers, and opened a book, glancing up at us every once in a while. She hadn't been in the gym long when Coach lined us up on the baseline. We had just finished running.

"Take a breather," he said. "We're gonna do it again in one minute."

"Again?" Khalil gasped.

Coach nodded. "Again."

"I'm gonna die before I see high school," Khalil grumbled.

We were seconds away from running when Megan came down and walked over to Coach. "Dad," she said.

"Yeah, Champ?"

"I was thinking . . ."

"Oh, great," said Roy.

Megan ignored him. " . . . Your next game is against Madden Creek. They're the biggest team in the league and you haven't worked on rebounding or boxing out since the first week of practice. Don't you think that might help more than just running all day? I mean, these guys aren't going to be any good if they're dead."

Trashman nodded and said, "She's right about that. Gotta be alive to take out the trash."

Coach looked down at Megan, then at us on the baseline. The whistle fell from his mouth. "All right," he announced. "Get in groups of three. A shooter, a rebounder, and one of you boxing out. Go!"

After that, nobody had a problem with Megan.

Our next game was Friday at Madden Creek. Madden Creek had a bad reputation. Their players were thugs. Their coaches were thugs. Their cheerleaders were thugs. The thing about facing a team of hooligans and goons was that whoever was playing them eventually became hooligans and goons, too. By the fourth quarter against Madden, the game had become a full-blown brawl, especially in the paint. Anyone who dribbled below the free-throw line was hammered instantly. For once, I was actually happy to watch from the end of the bench. The worst thing that happened to me on the sideline was a punch in the shoulder from Megan every time the ref called a foul.

"That was a *charge*," she said, socking me in the arm. Ruben had just been called for his fourth foul. One of the Ram guards had plowed into him while driving the lane. To add insult to injury, the basket was good, and Madden was up by six with five minutes to play. As far as we knew, our season was five minutes from being all but over.

Ruben fouled out a minute later. Then Roy. Then McKlusky.

"Malcolm!" Coach hollered. "Go in for McKlusky!"

Malcolm, aka Trashman, jumped up. "It's time to

take out the trash," he said as the home crowd egged him on.

We were down four now. There were three minutes left.

"Their best player has four fouls," said Megan. "We need to take it right at him. If they lose him, they'll lose the game."

It was hard to share Megan's optimism.

Then, with three minutes left in a five-point game, our tenth man fouled out. Coach had no choice. I was the last bullet in his chamber. He looked down at me and pulled the trigger. Momentum carried me right onto the court. Luckily, Megan grabbed me and pointed toward the scorer's table before I could make the same mistake again. "You have to check in, *pinerider*," she said.

"Oops."

"And take off your warm-up shirt."

My time on the court in the Hamilton game had been short, confusing, and, since the Harriers had been up by nineteen, meaningless. Now there was no more messing around. This was a game we could win— a game we *had* to win. And Coach was depending on me to step up.

We had the ball and trailed by seven. Raj was back in the game and playing with three fouls. He began the motion. My job was to set a baseline pick for JJ, who would use it to curl open in the opposite corner. The defender raced toward me, his eyes watching the ball. He was burly and had spikes gelled in his hair. One of his teammates called out, "Screen right!" but it was too late. Spikes slammed into me. I kept my hands at my side and didn't give an inch. On contact, Spikes brought his arm down hard on my thigh. Pain shot up my leg from the charley horse. The ref never saw the cheap shot. But JJ made his shot and we went the other way, needing a stop. We were down by five points with two minutes left.

Thirty seconds later the score was the same when Raj missed a long shot. The ball came off the rim straight into the hands of the Rams' point guard. I was the only person between him and the hoop. It was life or death for us. One more basket and the game would be out of reach. I shifted into high gear and raced to get in better defensive position. Knowing a touch foul would put Madden Creek on the free-throw line, I resisted the urge to swipe at the ball and came to a spot just off the right elbow.

The point guard was speeding straight at me with Spikes on the wing. Spikes had a glint in his eye. I knew that look. It said, *I'm going to score and there's nothing you can do about it because you are unworthy and I am great.* Sure enough, Spikes called, "Trailer," and the point guard dished. I shifted to my right and anchored myself to the floor. Spikes picked up his dribble and barreled toward me like a hurricane about to make landfall. I thought about Old Dude and the meaningless bloody lip he got when the game was already as good as won. If he could take one for the team during garbage time, I could do it now. Spikes went up. My arms were crossed in front of me. My feet set in concrete. His knee hit me first—right in the gut. Then his forearm hit my chin. Our hips collided and we tumbled to the floor. The last thing I saw as my vision faded to black was the ball falling through the basket. The Rams cheered. Our season was over. The whistle blew. A moment later JJ, Coach, Megan, and most of the team were standing over me. I tasted something warm on my lips. As I lay there on the court, the gym was as quiet as a church.

The cheer started from somewhere near the back of the bleachers. "Toh-BEE. Toh-BEE. Toh-BEE." It got louder. They chanted my name and stomped until Coach pulled me to my feet. "Way to go, Wheeler!" he shouted into my ear.

"Huh?" My head was still swimming.

"The ref called charge!" Raj explained excitedly. He handed me a tissue for my lip.

Ruben pulled me by one arm. The guys who were in the game surrounded me, high-fiving me and patting my head. JJ was there too, tapping my fist with his. And maybe it was the dizziness, but for a split second, I felt like we were back at the rec center and he was congratulating me for hitting a shot.

Over on the sideline our bench was going bonkers. Even Roy was waving a towel over his head. Behind them, the crowd was now cheering "Let's go, Chuckers!" We were still down five with a little over a minute to play.

Raj set up the offense quickly. There was no time to waste. We ran a high screen for JJ, who found himself doubled by his man and Spikes, the guy who was supposed to be guarding me. I knew what was coming. I raised my hands just in time to catch the ball, squared my feet, elevated, and released just as Spikes collided with me.

The whistle blew.

Two shots!

I stood on the free-throw line. Had someone pushed the hoop farther away or was it still just fifteen feet? I dribbled twice, then shot, using my right hand to push and left hand to guide like Megan and Coach had taught me. It was short. I looked over at the bench. Megan was mouthing something. "Bend your knees," she said.

I stared at the hoop and felt the crease of the ball in my hands. Then I bent my knees and released. The next shot was perfect.

We were down four.

Then Raj, who had been hiding behind Khalil, jumped in front of the inbounds pass, stole it, and zipped the ball to Malcolm under the basket. The lead was two!

"Pressure, pressure, pressure!" Coach yelled. "No fouls!"

We set up our trap. The Rams were rattled. The momentum was ours. Soon, the ball was too. There were ten seconds left. Raj yelled "Pilchuck!", passed off to JJ, and set a pick for me. Seeing JJ hounded by his defender, I shifted up to his right. We were beyond the three-point arc now. JJ dribbled toward me, leading his man right into the screen. Then, in the two seconds he was open, JJ drained a three-pointer as time ran out, and the gym erupted.

We lifted JJ up to celebrate. It was the same scene I had witnessed the year before—only now I was in the middle of it.

· 22 ·

All week, a smile was etched on my face. I hadn't been this happy since Megan and I beat Vinny Pesto at the rec center. Not even the extra set of wind sprints Coach ordered when Roy pulled Malcolm's shorts down in the middle of practice could kill the high. As a team, we were on the board—no longer winless—and I had made a difference. Sure, I was part mascot, part player, but at least now I mattered. And I was determined to make the feeling last. I was going to go to every game ready to do whatever I had to to help the team win. I would take a hundred charges, set a thousand screens, or just cheer from the end of the bench.

Wednesday was the night Raj, McKlusky, and I were going to the girls' game. I raced home from practice, showered, and bolted through the kitchen, where Dad was sitting at the table with a stack of books. I could see that the books were nothing I'd ever want to read. Some were about wood products. One was about writing business plans. But the books must have been interesting to Dad because when I slowed down to tell him where I was going, he barely lifted his head.

At the game, I found Raj and McKlusky. We cheered in the stands. After everything Megan had done to help me, it felt good to do something for her. Besides, she was right. The girls' team was good.

McKlusky was cheering more loudly than anyone. Every time Melanie drove the lane, he'd say, "You can't stop *that*." Then she'd hit a short floater and he'd say, "Can't stop that, either." Raj was quieter. Every once in a while, he'd mutter, "After the game. After the game I am going to ask Cassandra to the dance." He made at least six trips to the bathroom during the second half, and after each trip, he'd come back to his seat with his hair just a little different. Once, he came back without the turtleneck he had been wearing under his sweater. Five minutes later, he was back in the bathroom. When he reappeared, the turtleneck was back on. As the clock ticked down, Raj began tugging at it, like he needed air.

"Is it me?" he asked us. "Or is it hot in here?"

"It's you," I said.

"Gee, thanks."

"You have nothing to worry about," I promised. On the court, Megan stepped to the line. After she made the first one, the team huddled around her. "I guarantee you Cassandra is going to say yes."

"Why do you say that?" Raj asked as if I was holding out on him. "Do you know something? What did you hear?"

Megan missed the second shot. They were down two with two minutes to play. But Melanie stole the in-bounds pass. McKlusky stood and shouted to the other team, "Better call the police. You just got robbed!"

I wanted to watch the game but I had to calm Raj. He was a wreck. "I don't know anything," I said. "I just have a feeling. I saw the way she said hi to you in the woods. That wasn't acting."

"Maybe," he said.

"When you ask her, just be yourself."

"*If* I ask her. I might chicken out."

"You're not going to chicken out," I said.

Suddenly, everyone around us rose to their feet. McKlusky grabbed Raj and shook him. "Are you watching this?" he yelled. "Cassandra just tied the game!" Before Raj could answer, McKlusky was cheering again.

"Why is he so calm?" Raj asked.

"Probably because he isn't thinking about it."

As we watched Cedar Crest bring the ball upcourt with a minute left, I realized I was a little jealous of Raj. Sure, he was nervous about asking Cassandra. But at least he had decided to give it a shot. I couldn't bring myself to do more than *think* about asking Megan. What was I so afraid of? Not her dad. I didn't have that excuse anymore. Embarrassing myself on the dance floor? Maybe, but seeing McKlusky jump up and down like a lunatic after Cedar Crest turned the ball over made me suspect I might not be the only person in school without rhythm. As the girls' bench cheered on the starters before the last shot, it occurred to me I had been here before. It was something I wanted to do but always found excuses not to do—like join the basketball team. Well, this time I wasn't going to wait two years to get in the game.

The winning shot was a simple pick-and-roll from Melanie to Cassandra for a layin as time ran out. The crowd went crazy. I saw Coach Applewhite throw his fist in the air. The girls high-fived Cassandra, then scrambled to the locker room after shaking hands with the other team. With all the excitement, the temperature in the room had gone up ten degrees. While we waited for the girls to come back to the gym, Raj made one last trip to the bathroom. When he returned, the turtleneck was gone—again.

He and McKlusky waited near the snack stand by the front door. I sat in the empty bleachers. When Cassandra and Melanie emerged, Raj inhaled deeply. I could see he was talking to himself. He knew he had to go first. The girls walked up to them, smiling. Raj looked up at Cassandra, wringing his hands. Then, before anyone knew what had happened, McKlusky was talking to Melanie. He finished and she nodded enthusiastically. After that, it was only another second before Raj played his hand too. Cassandra beamed. When it was over and the girls had left the gym, McKlusky and Raj shook hands, then strode back to me, heads held high.

A moment later, Megan came into the gym, wearing track pants and a sweatshirt. I waved to her, but she didn't see me. Before I could walk over, Coach had her wrapped in a bear hug. Her mom was there too. I sighed. The timing wasn't right. If I was going to ask her to the Winter Blast, it wouldn't be today.

Ever since I made that free throw in the Madden Creek game, I had been looking forward to scoring an actual basket. It happened in our next game—against the other team's twelfth man. It was our fifth game of the season and afterward we were 2–3. The game was a blowout. McKlusky was leading the way with thirteen points, and he was 4–4 from the line, which just about made Coach tap-dance down the sideline.

As the time came off the clock and our lead increased, I slid farther and farther over the edge of my seat. Whenever play stopped, I looked to the other end of the bench, hoping Coach would call my name. He had put in everyone else, even Malcolm.

Finally, with 1:10 remaining, Coach called my name. I got into position on the court. When play started again, I lost my man behind a screen, caught the ball above the free-throw line, and, without hesitating, popped in a sixteen-footer that got nothing but net. It was one of the best moments of my life.

The next week was another home game. Coach tried

to put me in with two minutes left. I kneeled below the scorer's table and waited for a time-out or a foul or for the ball to go out of bounds—anything to stop the clock. But it never happened, and the buzzer blew with me still on the sidelines. That was life for a bench-warmer.

All along, we watched the standings closely. The top four teams would make the tournament. As winter break began, Hamilton and Madden Creek were locks. Menzel Lake was in third place. Twin Falls was in fourth place with us breathing down their necks. We would play them in the last game of the regular season.

It was all coming together.

And then JJ disappeared.

· 23 ·

I didn't see JJ at all during the two-week break. I played Risk in Raj's basement and shot baskets by myself on our street. Once or twice I heard the sound of a guitar and drums coming from JJ's house. Otherwise, there was no sign of him.

JJ wasn't the only person who was suddenly harder to spot than Bigfoot. Dad had become a workaholic. He stayed late at the office a lot and came home with stacks of files. I think Mom and I were thinking the same thing: he had to be the hardest-working wood chip salesman in the world.

Then, on the first day of school in January, Coach asked us if anyone had seen JJ. I kept quiet, but someone else said JJ had been in social studies. Coach raised an eyebrow, then blew his whistle and said, "Layups." That was Monday. The next day practice began at three like always. We were stretching in the corner. Raj was explaining that the key to beating Twin Falls was breaking their press, which they used more than any other team in the league. "If we can break them down, we'll have a lot of easy baskets."

"Forget about Twin Falls," said Ruben. "We have to take it one game at a time. This week the only team we have to worry about is Prospect Heights."

Roy waved his hand. "Prospect Heights—they stink. We'll beat them easy."

"Don't you know that's how upsets happen?" Ruben said. "One team thinks the game is going to be easy and the other team—the one that was supposed to roll over and die—catches them off guard."

"Come on, Ruben, they haven't won a game all year. There's no way they're going to beat us."

"Well, nobody thought we would have a chance to make the playoffs after starting 0 and 3, either. So you better come ready to play on Friday. We're going to need everybody."

"Speaking of everybody," said Khalil, "where *is* JJ? Is he sick?"

Roy was trying to spin a ball on his finger. "I say we can win without him. It doesn't seem like he ever cared that much anyway."

"Let Malcolm take the shots, baby," said Malcolm.

"Shut up, Trashman," Roy said. "Wait until you're spoken to—like a good rookie."

Everyone laughed. Except Malcolm.

"Look," said Ruben, "JJ may not be Mr. Emotional, but he did win a couple of games for us. I say we find out the real story, then make up our minds about what to do."

While this was happening, I was standing back, trying to keep a low profile. If the other guys wanted JJ on the team, that was up to them. Personally, I was ready to win with him or without him.

"Toby lives across the street from JJ," McKlusky said.

I shot a look at McKlusky.

It was too late, though.

"Hey, Toby," said Ruben. "Maybe you could stop by JJ's house after school. Maybe see what's going on. I'd talk to him myself during lunch or something, but he might take it better from a friend."

Well then, don't look at me, I thought. But I could see that this was not about me and JJ. This was about the team. I was going as an ambassador, not as anyone's friend. And I *had* promised myself I would do everything I could to help the team. If that included checking in on our star player, I would do it.

That evening, I puddle-hopped across Boardman street to JJ's house. When I knocked, the door creaked open. Lights were on in the kitchen and the living room. From somewhere in the back came the murmur and blue glow of a television. I opened the door. "Hello?"

No answer.

I walked into the kitchen.

"JJ?"

I went to the back of the house, thinking he had the TV on too loud to hear me, but the den was empty.

Finally, I heard voices upstairs. It was JJ and his father, arguing.

I should have left, but I inched up the stairs.

When I got to the top, I peered around the corner to catch an angle into JJ's room. His dad was standing in the doorway, holding something—a guitar.

"You are not going to waste any more time with this. Not until the end of the season. You will not skip another practice. Do you hear me?"

"Fine."

"This is your opportunity, JJ. And I'm not going to let you blow it over some stupid band. You got that?"

JJ raised his voice. "Okay!"

"I'm serious. I don't want any more calls from your coach. Okay?"

Then the dam broke and JJ lost it. "You don't have to worry about that anymore!" he shouted. "I called Mom and she said I could come to California anytime I want!"

California?

His dad marched past me and disappeared into his bedroom. When the coast was clear, I turned to leave. I stumbled, though, at the top of the stairs, and JJ heard me. Coming into the hallway, he said, "Toby! What are you doing here?"

"I . . ."

JJ stormed toward me. "Get out of my house! Don't you know what privacy means?"

I followed him down the stairs. "Why haven't you been at basketball practice?"

JJ wiped his nose with his sleeve. "It's none of your business."

"You're wrong," I said. "When it involves the team, it *is* my business."

"If you want to be my friend, Toby, just leave now."

"I'm not here as your friend, *jerk*. I'm here as your teammate."

"You really want to know what's going on?" JJ asked, his voice cracking.

"Yes."

"What's going on is that I'm quitting. I'm quitting and moving to California."

"When?"

"As soon as I can. I'll hitchhike if I have to."

"Chicken," I said.

"What?"

"I said you're a chicken. You're too afraid to stand up to your dad and tell him you want to play in the band *and* play basketball, so you're just taking the easy way out and quitting. Admit it."

"Why do you *care*?"

"I did care but now I don't think I do. If you're going to be like this, I think I would rather lose without you than win with you."

"I'm not a chicken," JJ said.

"Yes, you are. And you're selfish too. If you want to stay on the team, stay on the team. If you want to quit, quit. I don't care either way. But just so you know, your band stinks!"

JJ had done the worst thing a teammate could do to his team. He had quit when we needed him most. And he had done it without telling us. Not only were we no longer friends, now we were no longer teammates, either.

I slammed the front door and left.

· 24 ·

The only thing we knew going into the game against Prospect Heights on Friday was that Coach had suspended JJ from the team until further notice. It was our second-to-last game of the regular season and even though Prospect Heights was not very good, there was one question on everyone's mind: Could we win without JJ?

Ruben stood on a bench in the locker room before the game. "Everything we got, we got here in this room," he said. "No more, no less. Out there," he said, pointing to the court, "all we got is a job to do. And we're going to get it done." He put his hand in the middle of the circle. Ten hands fell on top of his. We cheered, then took the court for warm-ups.

Prospect Heights never stood a chance. With one

less perimeter weapon, we focused on getting the ball inside. One extra cut, one extra screen, and one extra pass on each possession, and we were a new team. Coach Applewhite set up a new play for the game. McKlusky set a high screen for Khalil, who passed to Roy on the wing, then rolled to the low block. Roy reversed the ball through McKlusky to Ruben. Normally, McKlusky would have followed the ball and set a screen for JJ. Instead, he set a down screen for Khalil, who took the pass from Ruben, waited for the defense, and dished to McKlusky for an easy two. The key was the pass from Khalil to McKlusky. The timing had to be right, the ball had to be at McKlusky's hands, and McKlusky had to catch it in motion and score without dribbling.

For my part, I waved my towel like a madman and knocked fists with McKlusky and anyone else every time play stopped. I was back on the end of the bench, but feeling good about the team and the way I was playing. We were coming together. We were going to be all right.

So when Coach Applewhite pulled me aside during practice on Wednesday, I thought he was going to ask me about JJ. Instead he handed me a white practice jersey and said, "I'm going to move you up in the rotation, Toby. Just for the next game. We're going to need every guard we have on Friday. And you've come a long way this season. Especially with your ball handling. It's time. Are you ready?"

"I'm ready, Coach," I said.

"Good," said Coach. "I'm going to sub you in when we need an extra guard on the floor. Sit closer to me on the bench, okay?"

"Got it."

I had come into the season dying to play in a game that mattered. Now I was getting my wish at last, and it scared me silly. But this was no time to back away.

On Friday, we played Twin Falls. Before the game, we got a surprise visitor.

Coach was making last-minute notes on the chalkboard when we heard a knock on the door of the locker room. JJ walked in, prodded by his father.

"I'll be with you in a minute," said Coach.

JJ's dad cleared his throat. "He's ready to play again."

I guess JJ wasn't getting out of Pilchuck as quickly as he'd thought.

Coach stared back through his glasses. "Not tonight, he isn't. Not for this team. He missed practice all week. If he wants to sit on the bench, that's up to his teammates. But he won't be playing."

"He's ready, Coach."

"I'd like to hear it from JJ."

JJ's dad pointed to Coach. "Say what you need to, son."

JJ was silent.

"*Say it!*" Everybody in uniform flinched.

Slowly JJ raised his head. The faraway look in his eyes was gone. He turned to his father. And he said what he needed to say. "I'm not playing for you anymore, Dad. I'll play for Coach and I'll play for these guys and I'll play for me, but I'm not playing for you. You took a game that was supposed to be fun and made me hate it. And if I never play again after this season, you can spend the rest of your life screaming about it." Then he said to Coach, "I'm sorry about what I did. If you'll let me, I want to play again. Not because I think you need me to win, which you don't, but because I want to help finish what we've started."

Coach looked at JJ. All season long he had sworn to us that if we ran our offense through JJ, we would be successful. Even when we were 0–3 and the rest of the team was on the verge of revolt, he had not budged an inch. Coach had put his faith in JJ and JJ had disappointed him. Was it JJ's fault for walking away? Was it Coach's fault for making more of JJ than JJ had wanted? Or was part of the deal, when you had a gift, that people expected a lot of you, even if you never asked them to? And would I really rather lose without JJ than win with him?

Eventually Coach broke the silence. "It's not up to me," he sighed.

Ruben spoke for us. "Coach is right. You aren't playing for us tonight. You disappeared on us. I'm sorry your old man got you all mixed up, but that can't excuse what you did. That's all I have to say."

Khalil nodded. "He's right."

"I'm with Ruben," said Roy.

"Me too," Raj agreed.

"Maybe next game," McKlusky added.

We went around the room like that until the circle reached me.

"Toby?" JJ asked.

I remembered thinking JJ had better hope there was never a time when he needed me. Well, that time had come. He needed me to speak for him. To tell the others he was a good guy, that he had made a mistake, that we should give him another chance. But I couldn't do that. He had not been a good friend to me for a long time and I didn't think I owed him anything.

"Sorry, man."

JJ looked at me the way I had looked at him the first day of practice, when the rest of the team had turned against me for missing that free throw. *Tough luck, buddy,* I thought as he and his dad left the locker room. But when I passed Coach on the way to the gym, the look he gave me made me think he could see right into the deepest part of my conscience, where I was already thinking, *Toby, that isn't you.*

The game was a nail-biter. It all came down to the fourth quarter. The score was tied. We were eight minutes from grabbing the final spot in the play-offs. The guys around me were breathing hard, red in the face, and holding on to the ends of their shorts for dear life.

Sitting down was the last thing on anyone's mind. I had been on and off the court all night. Coach would put me in for a play, then yank me back to the bench. "Wheeler, don't wait for the pass to come to you! Go to the ball!" The first time I went in, Raj told me to inbound the ball on the baseline. Twin Falls was in their 2–2–1 press, so Khalil was man-on-man at the other end of the court. Feeling bold, I decided to throw a deep pass straight to him. I thought he could catch, dribble, and shoot. I brought my arm back like a quarterback, and with all my might, chucked the ball forward. A second after I released, there was a *WHAM!* as the ball hit the back of the backboard and fell on my head.

But luckily Coach gave me another chance. With less than seven minutes left in the game, I caught an inbounds pass from Roy. The guy guarding me was my height, and quick, with arms like tentacles that seemed to reach everywhere at once. He was aggressive, too, and went after every ball as though his life depended on it. So when the pass came to me, I took the ball in both hands, raised it over my head, and snapped my arms forward like I was outletting to Ruben. Tentacles bit. He jumped just high enough for me to dribble around him. I could see the whole court as I weaved through traffic, past midcourt, and toward our basket. I kept my eyes on Roy, my wingman, but my mind was on Raj, trailing over my left shoulder.

Without shifting my glance, I flipped the ball behind me to Raj for a layin. We were up two. Then for good measure, I banked in a six-foot floater on our next possession. I hadn't felt this sure of myself on a basketball court since open gym.

Twin Falls called time-out with two minutes left. The game was tied.

I jogged to the bench with Raj, Roy, Ruben, and Khalil.

"Good work, Wheeler!" said Coach. "Take five. McKlusky, check in. They're staying small out there. Let's try to slow the game down. Use our size. If they trap, don't panic. Look for the good pass. Talk to each other!"

"Coach," said Ruben.

"What." It wasn't a question. Coach was in no mood for suggestions.

But Ruben spoke anyway. "You always say to feed the hot hand, right?"

Coach nodded impatiently.

"Well, Toby has the hot hand. Why would we go away from him?"

Coach tightened his grip on the clipboard.

Ruben pressed on. "You're always telling us to think for ourselves. Well, now we are."

Coach looked us each in the eye, then settled on Ruben. "Is that what you guys want?" he asked.

"Yes," said Roy.

"Okay." Coach nodded. "Khalil, you take a breather."

"Amen," Khalil puffed.

Coach smiled. "Don't ever let anybody say Coach Applewhite can't be reasoned with." Then he steeled himself and snarled, "Now get out there and win this game."

We traded baskets for the next three minutes. Twin Falls hit a couple of jump shots and converted a three-point play even though from what I saw, Ruben had never touched his man. I had to bite my lip to do it, but I kept my mouth shut as the ref passed by. On offense, Raj set a screen for me at the top of the key. With a pass from Ruben, I squared up near the free-throw line and sank a fifteen-footer.

But Twin Falls came right back. First they ran a pick-and-roll to pull within one. Then, on the inbounds pass, Tentacles wrapped his arm clear around me without making contact and batted the ball to his teammate. The basket was good and with the clock ticking under twenty, we were down one. Their bench was already celebrating. After all we had accomplished, would we really fall one point short of making the play-offs?

We were out of time-outs, so Coach waved to Raj to keep playing. He found Roy on the right wing. I set up on the low block, with Tentacles draped over me like a cheap suit. He was stretching for every ball that came my way. Roy saw it too. I cut toward him with my hands up. Roy pass-faked. Tentacles lurched forward as I switched directions on a dime. We passed each other in slow motion, him going one way with a helpless look on his face, me charging to the basket, taking the pass from Roy, and finishing for two.

We won. We were in the play-offs!

· 25 ·

Our first opponent in the play-offs was Menzel Lake. If we beat them, we'd be in the championship game.

Earlier in the season, they had come from behind to beat us in our own gym. Now we were on their turf.

Before the game, Ruben and the others cornered me in the locker room. Ruben had his arms crossed in front of his chest and a menacing scowl on his face. "You think you're something special now, don't you, Wheeler?" he asked. "That game-winner went right to your head."

"What do you mean?" I asked nervously, backing up against a locker. "What's going on?"

Roy stepped forward. "What's going on is that we're here to put you in your place, once and for all."

Even Raj pounded his fist into his palm. "It's what's best for the team," he said without expression.

Trashman shrugged. "They did the same thing to me, man."

"Think of it as an initiation," Khalil said.

"Has anyone seen Coach?" I asked.

"Coach has got nothing to do with this," Roy said.

I was lost. And outnumbered. "With *what*?"

"With this," said Ruben, reaching behind his back. As I braced myself, he held out a warm-up shirt, pulled it tight, and flipped it around so I could see what was written on the back.

" 'Pinerider'?" I said.

"It's your nickname," said McKlusky. "It was Megan's idea."

The breath rushed out of my lungs. I slipped the shirt over my jersey. It was official at last. I was the Pinerider.

"You earned it," said Ruben.

Megan beamed when she saw the shirt. We were on the sideline waiting for the game to start. The girls' season had ended. "It looks great," she said. "Dr. Dinkins would *definitely* approve."

"Thanks again for bringing me to see him," I said. "And for everything else. You really helped me a lot. Next year I promise I'll come to more of your games."

"*More* of my games?"

"Fine," I said as Megan admired the back of my shirt. "*All* of your games."

I thought about the dance next week. Tickets had

been on sale for a month. Raj had already taken his suit to the cleaners. McKlusky had even gotten his hair cut. But I had done nothing because I was a big chicken. *Bawk, bawk, bawk.*

I was feeling the beginnings of one of those just-close-your-eyes-and-do-it moments, when Vinny Pesto passed by on his way to the stands.

"Not sure if you saw the score from the early game, gym rat," Vinny said. "We won by twenty points."

The early game was the other semifinal. Hamilton had whipped Madden Creek to reach the championship game. The winner of our game against Menzel Lake would play Hamilton for the title.

"Enjoy it, Pesto," I said. "It was your last win of the season. We're gonna see you in the championship game tomorrow. And we're gonna mop the floor with you."

That was when Vinny peered down at my warm-up shirt. " 'Pinerider,' " he said. "What does that mean?"

"It means benchwarmer *extraordinaire*," said Megan.

"Perfect." Vinny nodded. "The little gym rat finally gets a nickname, and it's in French." He walked away laughing.

"I hate that guy," Megan said when Vinny was in the stands.

But there was no time to respond. And definitely no time to ask her to the dance. Raj hustled over to tell me it was time for the pregame huddle. As I made my way to the sideline, where the team had gathered around Coach, I took one last look into the stands. Mom and

Dad saw me and waved. Then, behind them, I spied JJ. He had slipped into the last row, where he stood and cheered as Coach began to speak.

"Remember the game plan. Run your offense. And stick with the box-and-one. Morelli, I want you physically attached to Gallagher all night. You got it?"

"Got it, Coach."

Then Ruben put his arm forward to the center of the circle. We all did the same. "This isn't the time for end-of-the-season speeches," he said. "Because there is no chance we are going to lose this game. You can try to lose it, but I'm not gonna let you. Just remember what Coach told us all season long. It takes twelve people to win a championship. Let's get it done."

We locked arms.

"Shock the world," said Ruben.

"Shock the world!" we repeated. "Shock the world!"

We were getting better at chanting.

Roy bottled up Gallagher and shut him down for three quarters. The rest of our players stayed in the zone. Going into the fourth quarter, we were up twelve.

Gallagher opened the quarter with a three, and the lead was nine.

Ruben missed a fall-away jumper.

Gallagher split a double-team and banked in a runner.

The lead was seven.

I watched the clock and bit my nails.

Raj walked the ball upcourt to eat up the clock.

Roy was fouled, but missed the free throw.

Menzel Lake's center put a drop step on Khalil, pivoted toward the basket, and dropped in a reverse layin.

The lead was five.

We were cold.

"We're playing not to lose," Megan said.

Sure enough, Raj, who earlier had been attacking the basket, looked tight with the ball now. With three minutes left, he did something out of character. He picked up his dribble along the sideline. Menzel Lake trapped him, forcing a turnover.

Gallagher drained a shot from the elbow.

The lead was three.

We had not hit a field goal all quarter. But we were in the bonus, so every time Menzel Lake fouled us, we got two free throws. Unfortunately, we were missing there, too. In fact, they were fouling Roy any chance they could because they knew he would miss.

There were less than fifteen seconds left. Menzel Lake held for the last shot. Then Roy made the biggest mistake of the season.

With seven seconds left, Gallagher was caught in the corner. All we had to do was contain him, let him put up a desperation shot, and head to Verlot Street for pizza. But Roy was in high gear defensively. When Gallagher raised the ball to shoot, Roy jumped up and in. The *in* was the problem. He made contact with Gallagher's elbow after the release. And when the ball went in, Roy collapsed.

On the bench, I covered my face with a towel.

Gallagher stepped to the foul line like he was going fishing on a lazy day. I guessed there was such a thing as being too calm, though, because the free throw was short. The ball hit the front of the rim, bounced twice, and fell into Roy's arms. Instantly, Roy was fouled.

Menzel Lake called time-out to freeze him.

Roy was practically sleepwalking when he reached the bench. He looked dazed and pale. The fact that we had fallen apart as a team in blowing a twelve-point lead no longer mattered. What mattered were those free throws.

"Snap out of it, Morelli!" Coach yelled, jerking at his tie. "This isn't over yet. You want to feel sorry for yourself, do it on your own time. For the next four seconds, you're still mine, got it?"

"Yes, sir."

Then Coach went over to talk to the ref.

We stayed in a huddle. Everyone looked nervous. Especially Roy.

"You can make it," Ruben told him.

"Yeah, yeah," he said in a fog.

The mood was so tense, I knew I had to do something. I grabbed Roy by the shirt and did my best imitation of Coach. "For crying out loud, Morelli!" I shouted. "How many times do I have to tell you there will be a game this season that will come down to free throws!"

McKlusky laughed. Trashman caught the bug next. After that it moved around the circle like a sneeze, until everybody was cracking up. As we broke the huddle, Roy shook his arms and rocked his head. He was loose. Well, looser.

I heard footsteps behind me. "For crying out loud, Wheeler," said a deep voice. Coach had heard me. But he was smiling. "Good work."

We got into position for the free throw as the crowd cheered. I heard "Miss it!" from one side and "You can do it!" from the other.

With three dribbles and an exhale, Roy pushed the ball out of his hands, through the air, onto the rim, and, as we watched from between our fingers, into the basket.

Could Roy make two in a row?

He aimed. And fired.

The entire bench had locked elbows.

The second shot was good.

"Roy!" Coach screamed at the top of his lungs to guard the inbounds pass. There were still four seconds left. Roy jumped up and down on the baseline like he had springs under his shoes. The pass was high but short, and the ball fell harmlessly to the ground as the buzzer blew, giving us the win and a spot in the championship game.

· 26 ·

Mom, Dad, and I celebrated that night. For once, we ate an entire meal without talking about Butte Peak or the effects of clear-cuts on spawning salmon. Instead we talked about basketball, and how Pilchuck was going to make history against Hamilton in the game the next night.

After dinner, Dad pushed back his chair and announced he had some news. My ears perked. Finally, we were going to learn his big secret. He stood with his chest stuck out and said proudly, "You are looking at the new director of retail operations for Landover Lumber!"

I didn't know what that meant, but it had a lot of words in it, and none of them were *wood chip* or *salesman,* so it had to be pretty good. Plus, Dad was glowing like he had just won the Super Bowl.

"Retail operations," Mom said. "I don't understand."

"We're opening a store downtown, Maureen! It was my idea. Well, I got the idea from Toby, but I wrote up the business plan and gave it to Warren. He loved it. See, all this time we've been selling our wood chips to the stores so they could sell them to customers. We're losing money on every sale! So I thought, *Let's sell straight to the customers—at the Landover Lumber store!*"

I smiled. "Straight to the hoop, Dad."

"And it's not just wood chips," Dad went on. "We're talking firewood, scrap wood, two-by-fours: a whole range of small-to-medium lumber byproducts for everyday use!"

Mom hugged Dad. "I'm so happy for you, Phil. Just as long as none of those lumber products come from Butte Peak, of course."

"Do we get a discount?" I was joking, but only because I was happy for Dad. His lightbulb moment had come. He hadn't gotten the promotion he wanted, but he had found a way to get in the game. He was off the bench.

The next morning, on the day of the championship game, I rode my bike over to the Applewhites'. I didn't call ahead. I just pointed my tires in the right direction and pedaled. I decided asking Megan to the dance had to be like pulling off a Band-Aid or jumping off the high board. If I thought about it too much, I would only psych myself out.

The ride across town was so cold, my fingers were freezing by the time I was halfway there. Megan lived in a brand-new house on a block that looked the same from one end to the other. There were hoops in every other driveway and about a million plastic reindeer. The Applewhites had a doormat with their name on it and a door knocker shaped like a basketball.

Coach answered the door. He was wearing pajama bottoms and an undershirt. "Wheeler," he said with a shiver. "What, um, why . . . why are you here?"

"Good morning, Coach," I said. "Is Megan home?"

Looking up and down the street, Coach said, "She went to the store with her mother."

"Oh."

"But come in. I want to talk to you anyway." He led me into a small office off the kitchen. The room was cluttered with boxes of videotapes, manuals, trophies, and team photos. A television sat on a filing cabinet across the room from the messy desk. Coach waved for me to sit on a worn couch.

"First of all, I want to tell you that I'm proud of you, Wheeler. I know the season didn't begin the way you wanted it to for yourself or for the team, but you hung in there, and you helped us accomplish something special. That's not always easy to do for someone in your position."

"You mean someone on the end of the bench."

"We've all been there, Wheeler. And we'll all be there again. Maybe not in basketball, but in some way."

"As long as there aren't any more wind sprints, anything is fine with me."

Coach chuckled. "I noticed you were silent the other night when JJ came into the locker room."

"Yes, sir."

"Aren't you two friends?"

"We were. Well, maybe we are. But I don't know anymore. He says he's moving to California. But he hasn't left yet."

"Is that why you stayed quiet?"

"Not just that," I said. "Ruben was right. JJ left the team. He can't just come back whenever he wants."

"We sure could use him on the court tonight."

"I know."

"But you're sticking to your guns? You think punishing JJ is more important than giving our team the best chance to win?"

Before I answered, I thought I heard the front door open and close. "I'm not the only one, Coach. The whole team feels that way. And I think we can win without him."

"I do too. But I also think that JJ made a mistake. One he regrets. And that maybe he deserves a break."

"Maybe."

"We all made mistakes this season, Toby. And all those mistakes were forgiven. It makes me think what we were doing—what we are doing—is more important than punishing each other."

"Are you saying you think JJ should play tonight?" I asked.

Coach replied, "I'm saying I want you to make sure that you're not using basketball to punish JJ for mistakes he made as a friend. If you really believe that JJ deserves to miss the championship game—a game we might not be in without him—then I respect your opinion. But if this is about something else, now is the time to do the right thing."

"Why me?"

"If not you, Wheeler, then who?"

We were quiet for a minute. Did Coach want me to leave? *Could* I leave without being excused? Technically we weren't in school. Coach said after a moment, "So, the big dance is coming up."

I nodded. *Now* I wanted to leave.

"Are you going?" he asked.

Deciding to come clean, I said, "That's sort of why I'm here. To ask Megan."

"You know, she's never been on a date before, Toby."

Suddenly, from just outside the room, I heard a gasp, then the sound of something hard, like a head, hitting the doorknob. A second later, someone cried "Ow!"

Coach opened the door and Megan spilled into the room, holding her head.

"Hi," she squeaked as she looked up, wincing. "I was just passing by."

"Hey, Champ," Coach said. "Guess what? Toby came over to ask you to the dance. It's just what you wanted."

Megan turned bright red. "Dad!"

"What? I'm saying you can go."

"Dad," Megan said. "*Toby* has to ask me."

"Oh, sure," Coach said, rubbing his chin. "Well, good. I have some work to do. Somewhere."

Coach had done the hard part. After that, it was just a matter of making the words come out of my mouth. I fumbled my way through it. I wasn't sure I had made any sense, but when it was over, I had a date for the Winter Blast.

I left the Applewhites' and rode home through the woods. I was still getting used to the idea that I had a date for . . . for anything. It was like wearing a new pair of shoes. Or waking up one morning and discovering I had wings. Still, the main thing on my mind was JJ. Maybe Coach was right. I was using basketball to punish him for mistakes he had made as a friend. That seemed especially unfair now that he had apologized to the team. JJ had hurt my feelings, and instead of getting over it, I was looking to make myself feel better through revenge, which, in the end, hurt both of us, and a lot of other people. In other words, I had become the selfish one.

As I turned onto Boardman Street, I was surprised to hear the sound of a basketball bouncing on the pavement. When I got closer, I blinked. JJ was shooting hoops—with Valerie! He was showing her how to shoot, except she kept pushing the ball, and every time it missed the rim, they would bust up laughing. Stephen was nearby on his skateboard, doing simple ollies along the curb.

"Hey, Toby," Valerie said when she saw me. "I heard you got a date for the Winter Blast."

Word traveled fast. "Yeah—I guess I do."

"Well, maybe we can all go together," she suggested.

Remembering Raj and McKlusky, I said, "I'll have to see you there."

Valerie shrugged, then, realizing her hands were covered in dirt, began searching for someplace to clean them. Seeing no good options, she went inside to use the sink in JJ's kitchen. Stephen was off doing drops from the back of an old pickup.

That left me and JJ. We stood in the middle of the street. Smoke rose from a house nearby and the wind carried the smell of burning pine. JJ ran a hand through his shaggy hair. My own nearly bald head felt suddenly cold.

"I was wrong," I said. "The other day in the locker room. I should have said something. But I didn't."

"I was wrong too. About the team. And a bunch of other stuff."

It didn't excuse what he had done, but it was nice to hear. Still, I wanted him to know the team wasn't begging him to come back, and neither was I. So I said, "We can win without you."

"I know."

I looked him in the eye. "Do you still want to play?"

JJ glanced at his house. "I'll be doing just what he wants."

"The way I see it, the only way to make this go away is to play. Because if you don't, he'll never let you forget it. But if you come out for one last game, you can walk away and there'll be nothing he can say about it, because you did it your way."

"What about the rest of the team?" JJ asked.

I knew how badly the team wanted to win. But I also knew they wanted to win as a team. Bringing JJ back just to take all the shots wouldn't accomplish anything—other than making Roy Morelli go out of his mind, that is. Still, I was certain now that we needed JJ on the court.

"What the rest of team wants is to beat Hamilton," I said. "Even if it means they have to hear you say you're sorry again."

· 27 ·

"What's he doing here?" Roy snapped when he saw me walk into the locker room with JJ on that Saturday afternoon.

"I'm here to play," said JJ. "If you'll let me."

"I thought we decided this already," Roy fired back. "We don't need him."

"Morelli," I said, "will you give it a rest? Did we kick you off the team when you almost cost us the first play-off game?"

"That's different," he said. But he backed off anyway.

Ruben stepped forward. "Roy has a point, Toby. We've gotten this far. Why should we take him back now?"

Everybody began speaking at once. Some of the guys agreed with Ruben and Roy. Trashman announced,

"Trashman doesn't care who plays as long as we win."
Raj yelled for quiet so I could talk. McKlusky banged
his shoe against a locker. I looked helplessly at JJ, who
seemed seconds away from turning and leaving for
good. Suddenly the door flew open and we heard a loud
whistle. But it wasn't Coach. It was Megan, standing in
the doorway with two fingers in her mouth.

"What's the matter with you guys?" she began. "The
biggest game of your lives is in ten minutes and you're
in the locker room arguing about whether your best
player should be allowed to play. Seems like a no-
brainer to me."

"We can win without him," said Roy.

"What are you, crazy, Morelli? Do you remember the
Landusky twins? They went for fourteen points *each* last
time you played Hamilton. They ran over you like logging trucks. And guess what? They've *grown*! Trust me,
the only way you guys are going to win this game is if
you can spread the court out. And the only way to do
that is to score from outside. So it comes down to this.
You can either act like a bunch of stubborn donkeys,
leave your best shooter off the court, and go on being
losers, or you can grow up, accept his apology, and stick
it to Hamilton once and for all." Megan stared us all
down.

Roy started to open his mouth.

Ruben shook his head. He reached into the equipment bag, dug out a jersey, and tossed it to JJ.

JJ slipped it on quickly. "Thanks for letting me back on the team," he said. "I never should have left."

"Forget about it, man," Ruben answered. "We got a game to win."

Coach came into the locker room. He saw JJ, smiled, and made a small check on his clipboard. Then he gathered us in a circle. "It's time," he began. "In thirty-two minutes, you guys are going to be league champions—if you remember what got you here. Twelve guys playing for something bigger than any one person." Coach swept his finger around the huddle like the second hand on a watch.

"Let's shock the world," Ruben said.

As the starters took the court, for the first time I laughed out loud at the thought of my being in the game with the clock ticking down. What had made me say that to Vinny? The odds were a million to one. In real life, I would be happy to win any way we could. As Roy passed me, I pulled him over and whispered, "If you watch Pesto closely, you can read him like a book. Whenever he curls his lip, it means he's going to shoot. When he takes a deep breath, it means he's going to drive."

"Thanks, Wheeler," said Roy. "I think I can use that."

Megan was right about the Landusky twins. They had grown. In fact, they were the tallest eighth graders I had ever seen. Combined, they were nearly twelve feet of muscle. When the two teams met on the court for tip-off, Pilchuck looked like Munchkins. Just before the ref blew his whistle, Vinny spied me, sneered, tapped his championship patch, and raised two fingers. I made the *L* on my forehead and got ready to cheer.

In the first five minutes, there were a combined eight turnovers, seven fouls, and four points. The Landusky twins were mugging anybody who came within spitting distance of the basket.

The game stayed close. With five minutes left in the third quarter, Coach called a time-out. I stood again, waving my towel and chest-bumping the guys coming off the court.

"We have to contain those guys inside!" Coach shouted.

Ruben nodded, wiping the sweat from his nearly bald head. "They're big, Coach."

Raj pointed to Ruben. "Your guy is putting the ball on the floor every time he catches it. Just stay low and wait for him to dribble."

After that, Ruben adjusted his defense. He waited for his man to catch the ball, kept his feet on the ground despite the head fake, and timed his swipe well enough to rack up four steals by the end of the third quarter.

Across the paint, Khalil and McKlusky were subbing in and out for each other and taking body blows from Hamilton's big men. Every possession was another round of hip checks, elbows to the gut, and forearms to the head.

On offense, JJ was slipping through defenders at will. Still, I wondered if anybody else could see he was holding back. Finally, in the fourth quarter, Megan said to me, "Why isn't JJ using his left hand?"

"Beats me," I said. Being able to go in either direction was one of the things that made JJ so dangerous. Why would he deliberately holster his secret weapon in the biggest game of the year?

The game picked up pace. Shots began to fall. JJ was smooth as ever. Pesto was hot too. Both offenses were clicking down the stretch. But the fouls were adding up—especially after the sloppy start to the game. Khalil sat with three fouls. Ruben picked up his fourth but Coach chose to leave him in. Then, with six minutes left in the game and Hamilton up by seven, Roy picked up *his* fourth foul. Kicking at empty space, Coach threw Malcolm into the game and told Ruben to stick with Vinny.

"Are you sure you want to do that?" Megan asked after the time-out. "One more foul and Ruben is gone."

"I know that!" Coach barked.

The ref blew his whistle and the game started again. There were five minutes left. Coming off a screen, JJ hit a three-pointer to pull us within four. Then Raj stole a lazy entry pass and skipped it ahead to Ruben for two more. Hamilton scored on their next possession; we answered back. It was a two-point game with two minutes to go, when Vinny curled his lip, jab-stepped, and fired a jumper. Ruben stretched his arm to defend, but he stretched too far and made contact. With a minute-forty on the clock, he was out of the game.

Coach called his last time-out.

"JJ," Ruben said, slipping on his warm-up shirt. "Your man is cheating to the right. You haven't gone left all night. The lane is there."

JJ shook his head. "Not yet."

Roy leaned in. "Come on, man! We're running out of time. Just go left."

"Not yet," said JJ.

Roy was about to protest when Coach cut him off. "It isn't gonna matter what anyone does on offense if you guys don't get a stop on defense!" He banged his clipboard against the top of a chair. "We did not come this far to fall two points short," he continued, picking up steam. "Pesto is *killing* us. We stop him, we win this game!"

"I can do it, Coach," I said.

Everybody turned to face me.

"I can stop him. I stopped him at the rec center. I can stop him here."

JJ nodded. "It's true, Coach. He can do it."

Coach stared at the rafters. "I can't believe I'm about to do this." Then he grabbed me by the shirt. "Start on the right wing. Set a screen for JJ. And, Wheeler—crash the boards. You got that?"

I felt a surge of energy rush through me. I was going to be on the court with the championship game on the line! As I took off my warm-up shirt, a roar came from the crowd. But I was focused on the job Coach had given me. Shut down Pesto. Set a good screen. Crash the boards. In a steady voice, I answered Coach. "Yes, sir."

Khalil inbounded the ball to Raj, who dribbled right to the top of the arc, passed to me on the right wing, then set a screen for JJ. It was the play we'd been running all season—and all night. JJ caught the ball and dribbled with his right hand. His defender stayed to his right, daring him to go left. Suddenly, when we absolutely needed a basket to stay alive, JJ went left. He switched the ball with a crossover, sped to the basket, and with his left arm extended, he delivered the ball to the rim, laying it in softly.

The game was tied.

The seven guys on the bench jumped up and down, hugging each other. But it wasn't over yet.

We raced to get back on defense. I found Vinny on the elbow. "Told you I'd be here, Pesto," I said.

"Not for long, gym rat. This game is over."

A moment later, Vinny had the ball. He was dribbling between his legs, but his eyes never left mine—and mine never left his.

"What're you gonna do, Pesto?" I asked. "Curl your lip and shoot, or take a deep breath and drive?"

Suddenly the smirk was gone. Vinny seemed unsure what to do with his mouth. So, at last, he chose to simply shut it. Dribbling left, he lobbed an entry pass into Melvin Landusky—the right-handed one. McKlusky was there, his red hair standing tall, his arms straight up and down. But the ref called a foul. The Hamilton bench erupted. Our fans booed loudly. With fifteen seconds left, the Harriers had a chance to go up two.

Landusky's first free throw hit the rim like a rock and shot straight back. The second one clanked against the metal hinge, bounced twice, and dropped in.

There was just enough time for me to find JJ.

"Pick and roll," I said. "If I set a screen and you roll with the ball, Vinny will stay with me. He won't switch. He'd rather lose than see me hit the winning shot in his face."

"You're sure?" JJ asked.

"One hundred percent," I said, remembering the play Megan and I had run at the rec center. "I've been here before."

JJ held out his fist—the ready sign. "One more thing," he said.

"What?"

"Game on."

I brought my fist down on top of his. "Game on."

We had to work quickly. Starting from midcourt, JJ dribbled toward me, leading his man into the screen.

Ten seconds left.

JJ's defender was stuck between me and JJ. I rolled the other way with my hands up.

Nine seconds.

JJ's man yelled, "Switch!" but Vinny followed me. There was nothing between JJ and the basket.

Eight seconds.

It happened in slow motion.

Vinny raced toward JJ, already blaming everyone else on defense for the breakdown.

Seven seconds.

JJ took the ball behind his back, looked one way, and passed the other way . . . to me.

Six seconds.

I caught the ball and paused, seven feet from the basket.

Come on, Vinny. Come and get it.

Pesto skidded to a halt, switched directions, and flew toward me. He wasn't alone. Three Harriers rushed at me. Out of the corner of my eye, I saw Raj open on the wing.

Five seconds.

When Vinny was close enough to see the whites of my eyes, I squared my feet, bent my knees, and swung a pass ahead of his outstretched hands.

Raj snagged it, pump-faked, and snapped an entry pass to Khalil.

Three seconds.

McKlusky flashed to the low post and Khalil hit him with the ball.

Two seconds.

Time seemed to stand still as McKlusky pivoted toward the basket and put the ball up off the glass.

I thought of Coach, who had given me a chance; Megan, who had been there too; Mom and Dad, who'd forbidden me to even think of quitting; Old Dude, who'd told me what a benchwarmer could be; and Vinny Pesto, who had lit the fire under me in the first place.

It had all come to this moment.

The ball bounced cleanly off the backboard and splashed through the net.

BUZZER.

The game was over and we had won. My world became a knot of sweaty bodies as twelve guys piled on top of each other in the paint. We were champions.

· 28 ·

The first person to find me after the game was Vinny Pesto. To my surprise, he was smiling. "You may be a champion, but you're still a gym rat to me," he said.

"Same to you, chump."

Vinny shook my hand. "See ya at the rec center, scrub."

There was only one thing to say. "I'm going to beat you like a twelve-egg omelet, Pesto."

For the first time, Vinny looked at me like he knew I could. Shaking his head, he said as he walked away, "I can't believe you passed the ball."

I was still charged with excitement as the court filled with people. Mom and Dad pushed their way through a pack of other parents and found me near the spot where, moments earlier, McKlusky had laid in the winning shot. Mom was fired up, like she had hit the winner herself. "That was amazing," she said as her feet danced on the hardcourt. "When does next season start?"

"Maureen," said Dad as he put his arm around me, "you're gloating."

"I don't care," she gushed. "We *won*, Phil. Toby won. I think we're allowed to enjoy it."

"We're very proud of you, Toby," Dad went on. "You found a way."

"I guess I had my lightbulb moment," I joked, before promising Mom and Dad I would meet them in the parking lot.

All around me, guys were still high-fiving and dog-piling. Across the court, Megan chatted with Valerie. The dance was the next night, but I wasn't nervous anymore. I knew there was a seventy percent chance Megan was going to be happy, no matter how many times I stepped on her feet. . . . The weather forecast was calling for snow.

Suddenly, I felt a large hand on my back. Coach Applewhite. He offered his hand—the same way he had that day we had met at the rec center. "We couldn't have done this without you, Toby," he said, his voice slightly hoarse from shouting. He leaned in. "The truth is I've always said it takes twelve guys to win one game, but I never *really* believed it until this season."

"Thirteen, Coach."

"Thirteen?"

"You always said it takes twelve guys to win one game. But it takes thirteen. You didn't count yourself."

Coach covered my hand with both of his. He released his grip, then left me near the baseline. I walked over to the bench. Down at one end, Coach's sport coat was still draped over his chair. Near the other end sat JJ, watching the rest of the celebration with a smile on his face. I took the seat next to him, the seat I had kept warm since November. He punched me lightly on the shoulder. Was he saying *good game*—or *goodbye*? I wasn't sure. But I knew that no matter what happened, it was okay now. He was free. And me? Well, I had proved to the world that a gym rat could play real ball, and that no one was too good for me. It was everything I had wanted to do. In fact, the only bad thing about the end of the season was how long I had to wait to do it all again.

Acknowledgments

Many thanks to the following people: Jodi, Elizabeth, Beverly, Vikki, Barbara, Maria, Ericka, Marissa, Joe, Victoria, Scott, and Chelsea.

About the Author

Thatcher Heldring grew up in the Pacific Northwest, where he taught himself to write and play basketball—though not at the same time. After college, he moved to New York City, where he played softball during the summers and indoor soccer year-round. In his spare time, he held down several jobs in book publishing. He has also worked as a grocery bagger, a ditchdigger, a shortstop, a small forward, a goalie, a scorekeeper, a coach, a rabid fan, and a benchwarmer. He and his wife, Staci, live in Seattle, a good place for indoor sports.

Thatcher Heldring's short story "A Genius for Sauntering" appeared in the young adult anthology *Not Like I'm Jealous or Anything: The Jealousy Book*, edited by Marissa Walsh and published by Delacorte Press. *Toby Wheeler: Eighth-Grade Benchwarmer* is his first novel. Visit him online at www.thatchertheauthor.com.